ZAC'S EVEN BIGGER HITS! VOLUME 2

BY H.I. LARRY

hardie grant EGMONT

Zac's Even Bigger Hits! Volume 2
published in 2018 by
Hardie Grant Egmont
Ground Floor, Building 1, 658 Church Street
Richmond, Victoria 3121, Australia
www.hardiegrantegmont.com

A CiP record for this title is available from the
National Library of Australia.

Front cover illustration by Jon Davis
Cover design by Pooja Desai
Back cover and internal illustrations by Craig Phillips
Internal illustrations inked by Latifah Cornelius

Printed in Australia by McPherson's Printing Group,
Maryborough, Victoria

1 3 5 7 9 10 8 6 4 2

CONTENTS

ZAC POWER

SHOCK MUSIC

CHAPTER

There must be a million CDs in this shop! thought Zac Power. *So how do I find the right one?*

Zac was in his local Tunes Super Store. And 'super' was the right word. It was so big you could get lost among the rows of CDs!

Normally, Zac just downloaded his favourite music straight to his SpyPad. But today he wasn't shopping for himself. It was his mum's birthday tomorrow, and she liked music on old-fashioned CDs.

Zac knew what kind of music he liked. The loud, rocking kind from his favourite band, Axe Grinder! But what about his mum? Zac had no idea.

Zac wished his brother Leon had made him a spy gadget that picked out birthday presents. Leon was always making gadgets because he worked for the Tech Division of the Government Investigation Bureau (or GIB for short). Zac also worked for GIB, but he went out on missions.

Zac loved being a spy, but it didn't help with buying presents.

Zac turned a corner and saw a huge stack of boxes. It was a display of red D-Pods, a new music player that he'd seen a few kids using at school.

The D-Pod didn't look that bad, but Zac had seen it up close and he could tell it was a cheap rip-off of the iPod.

Zac knew it would break a week after you bought it. *SO uncool,* he thought, looking closer. *Why would anyone want one?*

But as he looked around, he saw heaps of people wearing red earphones while they browsed. The D-Pod was catching on.

'Excuse me, sir,' said a voice from behind him. It was a Tunes staff member.

'Perhaps your mum would like this CD?'

The man held out a CD. On the cover it said *Twenty Trumpet Classics*.

Zac shrugged. He'd never heard his mum say she liked trumpets before.

Hang on, he thought. *How does this guy know I'm shopping for my mum?* Zac looked closer at the man's name tag. It said:

HELLO. MY NAME IS **GEORGE IAN BOB.**

What a weird name, thought Zac. *Hang on, that spells G-I-B!*

The man winked and said, 'You really should hear this CD, sir. Why don't you listen to it on those headphones over there?' He pointed to a corner of the shop.

Zac took the CD over and popped it in

the player. Then he put the headphones on. Immediately, he felt an itchy tickling in his ears, like something was crawling in.

Ew, thought Zac. *This must be a GIB Wax Scanner!* He tried to keep still as the scanner checked his unique earwax pattern.

Finally he heard a little beep in the headphones. A message came up on the CD player:

ID CONFIRMED.
Welcome, Agent Rock Star!
Ejecting GIB mission disk now.

The CD player opened. Instead of the CD Zac had put in, there was now a shiny little GIB mission disk. Cool!

Zac knew the disk would slot into his

SpyPad, the all-in-one super-gadget that every GIB agent carried. But he couldn't use it in public. He needed to go somewhere private.

Mum's present will have to wait, Zac thought, nodding at the GIB agent and heading for the exit.

But when he crossed into the next aisle, he could barely get through. The aisle was filled with people wearing red D-Pod earphones.

'Excuse me,' Zac said, tapping one of them on the shoulder. It was a teenage girl. 'Can you let me through, please?'

The girl turned around. Her eyes looked a little glazed. 'This D-Pod is so cool,' she said in a robot-like voice. 'You should totally buy one.'

'Yeah,' droned another guy. 'The D-Pod is amazing.'

I don't have time for this, Zac groaned to himself, trying to dodge around the crowds. But people kept shuffling into his path.

Then Zac's spy senses started tingling. *Something's wrong,* he thought. *Everyone who's wearing the D-Pod earphones is acting like a zombie!*

The crowd was now surrounding Zac. They were all shuffling sleepily and mumbling things like, 'D-Pods are awesome.'

Some of them were trying to put the earphones in Zac's ears!

Zac backed up against a huge stack of boxes. *I've got to get out of here!* he thought. *But how?*

CHAPTER 2

Zac felt the boxes digging into his back as the crowd stumbled closer.

There was only one way to go, and that was up!

Luckily Zac had done a lot of karate training in spy school, so he knew how to get out of tight spaces. He took a deep breath, bent his legs and then kicked off the ground with all his might. He leapt into the air and back-flipped over the stack of boxes, landing on the other side. Then he pushed the boxes over, scattering them on the floor.

CRASH!

That should hold the crowd back for a few moments, Zac thought, sprinting for the door as the zombies tried to shuffle over the boxes.

On the street, Zac saw more people wearing D-Pods. They were dragging their feet as they walked, mumbling about how great D-Pods were.

It was kind of creepy, like the old zombie movies Zac had seen on TV.

What is WRONG with them? thought Zac. *Maybe it's something to do with my mission.*

But before Zac could even reach for his SpyPad, he heard screeching wheels.

A moment later, a stretch limo spun around the corner and pulled up next to him. The sun roof rolled open and Leon stuck his head out.

'Zac, what do you think of the D-Pod?' he yelled. 'Tell me, quick!'

'Er – I think it's ugly and creepy,' called Zac. 'Leon, what are you doing here?'

Leon sighed with relief. 'Good, you're not a zombie. Get in!'

Zac pulled open the door and slid into the limo. Inside, there were panels covered in blinking lights, levers and computer displays.

Leon was sitting up one end, surrounded by screws and bits of D-Pods that had been taken apart.

'This is our new CamoSine,' explained Leon, as the limo took off automatically down the street. 'From the outside it looks like a limo, but it's way more useful than that. It's on autopilot at the moment. Have you read your mission yet?'

Zac shook his head. 'But what kind of mission needs a limo?'

Leon gave him a quick grin. 'You'll see in a minute.'

Zac slid the disk into his SpyPad.

CLASSIFIED

MISSION INITIATED: 6 P.M.
CURRENT TIME: 6.30 P.M.

GIB has discovered that the D-Pod, a popular and very cheap music player, is actually a mind-control device. The D-Pod turns its users into 'zombies', who go around convincing other people to buy D-Pods.

GIB suspects that the evil scientist Dr Drastic is behind the D-Pod. Unless a cure can be found in 24 hours, the zombies will be under Dr Drastic's control forever.

YOUR MISSION:

Reverse the zombie mind-control process before it's too late!

~ END ~

Zac looked up at Leon. 'The D-Pod is turning people into zombies? But how?'

Leon looked tense. 'The D-Pod comes with one free song already loaded onto it,' he explained, holding up half a D-Pod. 'The song has a built-in mind-controlling sound pattern called a Zeta wave. When you listen to the song, the Zeta wave sort of fries your brain.'

'And it makes you go around telling other people to buy the D-Pod,' Zac finished.

'That's right,' said Leon. 'The D-Pods are cheap, so everyone's buying one. By this time tomorrow, Drastic could have thousands of people under his control!

But that's not even the worst bit.'

Zac snorted. 'What could be worse than an army of zombies under Drastic's control?'

Leon cleared his throat. 'Er ... The mind-control song on the D-Pod is by your favourite band, Axe Grinder.'

Zac's mouth dropped open. 'No way!' he said, horrified.

Leon tapped at his controls and a song began playing inside the CamoSine. 'It's called *Brain Quake*,' he said. 'I've removed the Zeta wave, so it's safe to listen to.'

Zac felt sick, but he forced himself to listen. The song sounded weird. It wasn't like Axe Grinder's other songs at all.

It's almost like they're playing the notes in the wrong order, he thought.

'Terrible,' said Zac when the song had finished. 'OK, so how do we stop Drastic?'

'We go right to the source of the problem,' said Leon. 'And you might feel better once you hear the plan. You're going undercover as a rock star with Axe Grinder!'

CHAPTER

Zac almost fell off his seat. 'That is *awesome*!' he yelled.

'I know,' grinned Leon. 'They need a back-up guitarist for their gig at the MegArena tomorrow, so GIB arranged for you to fill in. Rehearsal is in the morning at Lux Hotel in Music City.'

Zac's stomach was flipping with

excitement. 'But Music City is on the other side of the world,' he said. 'We'll never get there in time if we drive a limo.'

Leon smiled. 'True,' he said. 'But the CamoSine isn't a normal limo. Take the wheel and flick those two switches.'

Zac settled into the driver's seat and turned off the autopilot. Next to the first switch was a small label that said 'Flight Mode'.

Zac flicked it, and a second later he saw wide, sleek metal wings sliding out from underneath the limo.

'Cool!' he said, and the CamoSine began picking up speed.

Zac adjusted a few more controls, and

the twin scram-jet engines roared as the limo took off into the air.

WHOOSH!

Lucky we're in a quiet street, thought Zac as they blasted into the sky. *It's not every day you see a flying limo!*

Once the CamoSine had levelled out at 30,000 feet, Zac set the autopilot to head towards Music City. Then he stood up from the controls and turned to face Leon.

'We should get to Music City in about twelve hours,' he said, flopping down on the CamoSine's leather seats. 'So, what kind of disguise kit have you got for me this time? A holographic suit? Nano-particle camouflage masks?'

But Leon shook his head. 'You're going undercover as a rock star,' he said, handing Zac a leather jacket and a pair of sunglasses. 'You just need to look cool! Although you'd better fix your hair – it's all messy.'

Zac rolled his eyes. His hair was *supposed* to look messy. Leon was such a nerd sometimes.

Leon pointed to the sunglasses. 'Those are SHADES, the Secret Highly Advanced Detection and External SpyPad system. You won't be able to use your SpyPad while you're undercover, but you can use these to contact me and GIB. They'll also identify any threats around you.'

'Cool,' said Zac. Then he caught sight of something hidden underneath the seat.

'Is that an electric guitar?' he yelled, jumping down and pulling it out.

It was heaps cooler than Zac's guitar at home – this was a top-model, shiny red Pender Straz. *Awesome!*

Leon rolled his eyes. 'Yes, that's for you too,' he said. 'Don't let it out of your sight. It's been upgraded with high-security features to keep you safe while you're performing. And here's your backpack – there's a few extra gadgets in there you might need.'

The backpack was covered in cool badges and a wicked drawing of a snake, but Zac was heaps more interested in the electric guitar. He couldn't wait to rock out with Axe Grinder on stage!

Leon seemed to guess what he was thinking. 'Don't forget, Zac – you're on a mission. You've got to figure out how to reverse the effect of the D-Pod before it becomes permanent.'

Zac nodded, trying to look serious. Then he remembered something important. 'Leon, what's my rock star identity?'

'Oh, right!' said Leon. 'You're Tom Rocket, wicked guitar player and rocker. GIB have planted a few articles in the newspapers, so everyone will know he's Axe Grinder's new guitarist.'

Zac stood up and peered at himself in the mirror, checking out his leather jacket and making sure his hair looked right. 'Tom Rocket, huh?' he said, grinning. 'I like him already.'

Leon glanced over at the CamoSine's flight deck. Zac had almost forgotten they were still flying through the air.

'We've got hours before we get to Music City,' said Leon. He pulled a little book out of his pocket and held it up. 'Want to do some maths puzzles with me?'

Zac laughed. 'Tom Rocket doesn't do maths puzzles,' he said. 'What else is there to do?'

'Well,' said Leon, 'I suppose there's

this.' He pushed a button, and a huge LCD screen dropped down from the roof of the limo. Two games consoles popped out of the seat cushions. 'It's got pretty much every game ever made on it,' he explained.

Zac grinned. 'Now *that's* more like it.'

CHAPTER

It was early morning when the CamoSine's GPS beeped to say they were almost at Music City. Yawning after a night of playing games, Zac slipped into the driver's seat and guided the flying limo down.

They landed in a quiet area outside of town. Zac set the autopilot to head straight for the Lux Hotel, where he was supposed to meet Axe Grinder for rehearsal.

Zac stared out the window as they drove through the city streets. He could see heaps of people wearing the red D-Pod earphones, shuffling along and trying to get other people to buy them too.

Zac shuddered, remembering again that the free song on the D-Pod was by Axe Grinder.

I just can't believe they'd help Drastic to do something so evil, he thought. *There must be a another explanation.*

Zac saw the hotel a long time before they got there. The Lux Hotel was 100 stories tall and shaped like a rocket ship.

It was famous for being very expensive and exclusive. All the big stars stayed there when they toured Music City.

As they got closer to their hotel, the streets became busier and busier until the CamoSine slowed to a crawl. Zac caught sight of a group of people wearing black Axe Grinder T-shirts.

They must be fans here for the gig tonight, he realised. He glanced at his watch. 9 a.m.

We'd better hurry if I'm going to make my rehearsal, he thought. *I don't want to be kicked out of the band before I even play with them!*

Eventually, the CamoSine pulled up outside the Lux Hotel. A long red carpet led up to the hotel's huge revolving door.

The crowds on either side were screaming and waving their hands.

Leon turned to Zac. 'Good luck with your rehearsal,' he said. 'But I, er, forgot to mention one thing. Everyone knows who Tom Rocket is, but no-one knows what he *looks* like. So you'll really have to act like a rock star to get into Lux Hotel.'

Zac winked at him, rock-star style. 'No worries, bro,' he said. He leant over and flicked a switch marked 'External Speaker'. Now everyone outside could hear him.

'Ladies and gentlemen,' said Zac into the microphone in his deepest voice.

The crowd outside went quiet and

everyone turned to stare at the CamoSine.

'He's Axe Grinder's new guitarist,' Zac boomed. 'And he's the hottest new star in rock 'n' roll. You'll all go craaaaazy for ... **TOM ROCKET!'**

The crowd outside went wild as Zac flung open the door of the CamoSine, slung his guitar over his shoulder and leapt out onto the red carpet.

'Hi, everyone,' Zac yelled, striking a few chords on his guitar. 'Do you want to ROCK?'

The fans cheered even louder.

'I can't hear you!' Zac shouted, strumming his guitar.

Camera flashes were going off all

around him as the crowd roared. *This is so cool,* thought Zac. *They all believe I'm a real rock star!*

But then Zac caught sight of the four security guards standing at the top of the red carpet. They had their arms crossed and they were frowning. Then one of them muttered something to the others.

Zac knew they weren't convinced by his act. He'd have to do something really rock star to get into the Lux Hotel.

The crowd was still cheering for him. 'Play us a song!' someone yelled.

Good idea, thought Zac with a sly grin. He swung his guitar around and set it to AutoAmplify.

'OK, everyone,' he yelled. 'You wanna rock? Let's *rock*!'

Zac slammed down on the guitar. The crowd screamed with excitement as he started playing one of his favourite Axe Grinder songs.

GONNA HAVE TO ROCK YA!
ROCK MY WAY THROUGH!

As Zac played, the fans danced like crazy. He rocked out all the way down the red carpet, high-fiving Axe Grinder fans and finishing off with a wicked solo.

When he finished, he was standing at

the top of the stairs in front of the security guards.

The biggest guard leant forward and looked Zac up and down.

This is it, thought Zac. *If I get past this guy, I'm in. If not …*

He tried to send out strong 'I'm Tom Rocket' vibes.

The guard seemed to stare at him forever. Then finally he leant back, made a tick on a clipboard, and said, 'Welcome to the Lux Hotel, Mr Rocket. Your band is waiting for you inside.'

Zac gave him a grin, and then strolled through the big revolving door into the Lux Hotel. *I'm in!*

CHAPTER 5

Zac looked around the lobby of the Lux Hotel. *Wow,* he thought. *This place is seriously huge!*

The lobby was the size of a soccer pitch and full of fountains and statues, but the most impressive part was its ceiling.

It didn't *have* one. At least, that was what it looked like. The lobby was open all the way up to the penthouse suite, 100 floors above. It was so high you couldn't even see the top.

There was a reception desk far across the lobby. Zac could see a man in uniform sitting behind it.

'Hi, I'm Tom Rocket,' said Zac, walking over. 'I've got a rehearsal with Axe Grinder.'

'Ballroom number three,' said the receptionist snootily, pointing down a corridor. 'They're filming the rehearsal for a music video, so you'd better hurry.'

Zac's stomach flipped with excitement. *A music video!* He followed the corridor to a set of fancy-looking doors.

There was a sign hanging from the handles:

AXE GRINDER REHEARSAL
– FILMING IN PROGRESS –
NO electronic devices

Zac pushed open the door and was instantly blasted by music coming from inside.

GOTTA DO IT
GOTTA ROCK THIS HOUSE!

'Awesome,' Zac said under his breath as he walked inside. The room was as big as the lobby, but crammed full of Axe Grinder fans and cameras and bright lights. And at the far end was Axe Grinder, rocking out on stage!

No wonder they had security guards on the door, thought Zac. *All those fans outside would love to be in here!*

Zac was already late for rehearsal, but how was he supposed to get to the stage? There were people crowd-surfing and diving everywhere. It was a giant mosh pit!

First I should check for any D-Pod zombies, Zac remembered. He tapped his SHADES and set them to Scan.

SCAN MODE ACTIVATED
Zombies detected: 0

That makes sense, thought Zac.

The sign on the door had said 'no electronic devices', so the guards would have stopped anyone wearing earphones.

Now how am I supposed to get through all these people to the stage? thought Zac. He glanced at his watch. It was 10.07 a.m.

No time to waste. Zac opened his backpack to see what gadgets Leon had packed for him. He pulled out a stubby shape with a thick barrel.

A LaserLine! he thought. *Perfect!*

The LaserLine was like a portable grappling hook. It fired a thin, super-strong wire at a target, and then wound it back in. Good for bringing something closer to you, or bringing you closer to something!

Zac adjusted his electric guitar so that it was strapped safely to his back, and then aimed the LaserLine at the stage.

FREEEOOOOOWWW!

The invisible line whirred over the mosh pit and into the wall next to the stage.

THUNK!

It stuck tight. The wire now stretched from Zac all the way across to Axe Grinder.

Now for the quickest way across a mosh pit, thought Zac. *Over the top!*

Still holding the barrel of the LaserLine, Zac ran and took a flying leap onto the dancing moshers.

Then he hit the Retract button on the LaserLine and it quickly wound back,

pulling him towards the stage at top speed.

Everyone cheered as Zac flew over the crowd, waving and pushing him forward with their hands. He wasn't just LaserLining – he was crowd-surfing too!

Just before he got to the stage, Zac let go of the LaserLine and landed with a thump on the stage. Axe Grinder was playing right in front of him. Zac could hardly believe it.

The lead singer, Ricky Blazes, saw Zac and waved him over. 'Hey, you must be Tom Rocket!' he yelled over the music. 'Ready to play?'

Zac grinned and swung his guitar around. 'Am I ever!'

CHAPTER

The band rehearsed for hours, playing every one of their songs all the way through. Zac knew them all and kept up easily, though by the end his fingers were starting to get sore from all the strumming and plucking.

Finally, Ricky Blazes sang the last song and called it quits, motioning for the lights to come on. 'Thanks for coming, guys,' he told the fans. 'The music video will be out next month, so keep an eye out for it. See you tonight at the MegArena!'

Zac stretched as security guards started ushering people out. He felt stiff from hours of playing, but he'd never been so happy in his life!

'That was some pretty radical playing,' said someone from behind him. 'You like our music, Tom Rocket?'

Zac turned around. It was Ricky Blazes.

'Oh, well, you know,' said Zac, trying to be cool. 'I'm a bit of a fan.'

Ricky nodded. 'Thanks, man, that's great. Well, I'd better go get ready in our penthouse suite for tonight's gig. See you later!'

I've got to ask Ricky about the D-Pod, Zac thought as the star turned away. *By the time the gig starts tonight, it'll be too late to stop all those people from being Drastic's zombies forever!*

'Hey, Ricky,' called Zac. 'I was just wondering … What's with that D-Pod song you guys did?'

Ricky turned back to Zac. 'Oh, you mean "Brain Quake"?' he said. 'We just did it for the money. This guy DJ Draz paid us heaps to record this weird song he'd written. It was so bad it'd probably sound better if you played it backwards.'

DJ Draz? thought Zac. *That sounds a lot like Dr Drastic.*

'What does DJ Draz look like?' he asked casually.

Ricky smiled. 'He had this mad white hair and his glass eye kept popping out. That was sort of cool, actually. But he was kind of nasty so we didn't hang with him for long.'

That's Dr Drastic all right! thought Zac.

'Do you know where I could find DJ Draz?' he asked.

'Oh, sure,' said Ricky. 'He's over at –'

'Mr Blazes?' said a voice suddenly.

The security guard from outside had appeared at Ricky's elbow. 'There are some red boxes waiting for you at the front desk. The guy says it's urgent.'

'OK,' said Ricky. 'Listen, Tom, we've gotta go, but it was rad meeting you. I'll catch you at the MegArena!'

Zac sighed as the security guards escorted Ricky and the rest of the band off-stage. He'd had an awesome time playing with Axe Grinder, but he was no closer to solving his mission and saving all those people from being Drastic's zombies.

What do I do now? he thought, checking the time. It was 2.45 p.m. There were just over three hours until the gig started. Then everyone who owned a red D-Pod would turn into a permanent zombie.

Hang on a minute, thought Zac suddenly. *Did that guard say that someone had left RED boxes at reception for Axe Grinder?*

Zac gulped. Maybe they were D-Pods from Drastic!

He sprinted back to where he'd left Axe Grinder, just in time to see the elevator doors closing.

Ricky and the rest of the band were in one of the clear glass elevators. They were all holding red D-Pod boxes in their hands!

Zac groaned. *I've got to catch them before they put those D-Pods in their ears!*

He raced over to the elevator and pressed all the buttons, but nothing happened. Zac knew it would be too late if he didn't find another way to get to Axe Grinder's room.

Zac watched as the elevator started to rise inside the clear glass wall. *I'll just have to beat them to the top*, he thought. *Lucky I'm wearing AeroMasters.*

AeroMasters were one of Leon's new inventions — sneakers that came with built-in pressure suction so that you could walk on any surface. Even up walls!

Zac had never used them before. *These had better work*, he thought grimly.

Zac knelt down and set each shoe to Vertical Mode. Then he took a deep breath and started running up the glass wall.

THWOCK-THWOCK-THWOCK!

Zac's sneakers held tight to the wall as he raced up behind the lift.

THWOCK-THWOCK-THWOCK!

Within seconds he'd almost caught up, but just as he did he caught sight of Ricky Blazes opening the D-Pod box. The other band members were doing the same thing.

THWOCK-THWOCK-THWOCK!

'Stop!' he yelled, but Ricky couldn't hear him.

Zac tried to go faster, but he was too late. Just as he got to the top floor and leapt over the balcony, the elevator door dinged and all the Axe Grinder band members shuffled out wearing red earphones.

'Hey, Tom,' said Ricky Blazes sleepily. 'These D-Pods are rad – and we've got one here for you!'

Oh no! thought Zac. *Axe Grinder have turned into zombies!*

CHAPTER 7

Zac backed away as the members of Axe Grinder stumbled closer. *This mission is turning into a disaster,* he thought. *What am I going to do now?*

Zac ducked into the penthouse suite. The place was amazing. It had a pool table, guitars everywhere and its own helicopter outside on the helipad.

But there was no time to enjoy it, because Zac could hear Axe Grinder coming in after him. He quickly hid behind a plant.

The band shuffled into the room, mumbling to each other.

'This D-Pod is totally awesome,' Ricky murmured.

'I love my D-Pod,' said the drummer. 'Everyone should have a D-Pod.'

Then Zac heard a familiar voice coming from the next room.

'Is that my favourite band?' said Dr Drastic, walking in with a nasty grin on his face. 'Hello, boys!'

Zac shuddered. He'd met Dr Drastic

heaps of times, but the evil scientist still gave Zac the creeps. He ducked behind another pot plant, trying to stay out of sight.

'Hello, DJ Draz,' murmured the Axe Grinder band members, wandering over to Dr Drastic. 'You should buy a D-Pod. They are amazing.'

Drastic rolled his one good eye. 'I hope my other zombies aren't as dumb as you,' he muttered. 'But at least now you won't keep asking about the Zeta waves I laid over "Brain Quake".'

Zac breathed a quiet sigh of relief. He'd known deep down that his favourite band wouldn't have helped Drastic make something so evil. But he was glad to have it confirmed.

'You were always asking stupid questions,' Drastic was ranting. 'Always making suggestions about how to improve "Brain Quake". The song is an instant classic just the way it is – and it had to be that way to support the Zeta wave.'

The Axe Grinder zombies just stood there.

Suddenly Drastic stopped, and laughed madly. 'But none of that matters now, Axe Grinder!' he grinned. 'I've sent a message to all my zombies to come to your concert tonight. By the time you finish the first song, the effects of the mind-control process will be permanent – and I'll have a whole army of zombies under my control!'

The Axe Grinder zombies watched as Drastic giggled. Zac saw that the drummer was even drooling a little bit.

Drastic sighed happily. 'Now, my zombies, hurry up and get in the chopper. We're going to make our final preparations for the concert tonight. Let's go!'

They're headed for the MegArena early, Zac realised, glancing at the time. It was 4.05 p.m. There were only a couple of hours before the gig! Zac had to get on that chopper with Drastic and the zombies, or else he'd never make it to the MegArena in time.

Zac followed Drastic and Axe Grinder towards the helipad. He made sure he kept well-hidden behind the door until they were all on the chopper.

Can't get in with them, thought Zac, thinking hard as the chopper's blades started spinning. *They'll just turn me into a zombie! But I need to stick with them somehow.*

Then Zac saw the long landing skids on the bottom of the helicopter. *I could hang on under there,* he thought, adjusting the strap of his guitar so that it sat snugly against his back. *But I'll have to time this perfectly!*

The helicopter blades were turning faster and faster, and within moments the chopper had lifted off. Before it could get too high, Zac raced across the helipad and leapt into the air, grabbing hold of the chopper's landing skids.

As the chopper lifted higher, Zac used every muscle in his body to pull himself up to sit on the skids. He held on tight as the chopper picked up speed.

Phew! thought Zac. *Half a second later and I'd be a pancake down on the red carpet!*

The helicopter flew across Music City with Zac hanging on underneath. It was a short flight, but to Zac it felt like forever. Cold wind whipped around his body, and soon he could feel his teeth chattering.

Not long now, he thought, shivering.

Sure enough, the huge MegArena Stadium appeared in the distance a few minutes later.

As the chopper flew closer, Zac could see crowds of people lining up outside. They were shuffling along in a way that was horribly familiar.

His SHADES scanned the crowd.

SCAN MODE ACTIVATED
– ALERT! –
Zombies detected: 4000

Zac groaned. He didn't have long before all those people became Drastic zombies forever!

Then he remembered something else. He had get off the chopper before it landed, or he'd be caught and turned into a zombie!

Zac gulped. There was only one way to get off the chopper. And that was straight down …

CHAPTER

Zac stared as the MegArena loomed closer. He'd jumped from great heights before, but usually he had some kind of parachute.

Still shivering from the cold, Zac reached around slowly for his backpack to see what else Leon had given him.

Surely there's something in here I could use

to get down safely, he thought, rummaging as carefully as he could without letting go of the landing skids.

Then Zac pulled out a stretchy rubber outfit. *Oh, sweet!* he thought. *A prototype Human Super-Ball.*

The Human Super-Ball was a loose bag that you put on over your clothes, and when inflated it blew up into a person-sized rubber ball. It was perfect for bouncing from a great height or across long distances.

The only part Zac didn't like was the way you made the Super-Ball deflate again. Leon could only get the rubber to dissolve with human saliva — so if you spat in it, the Super-Ball would turn into a gooey mess within ten seconds. Gross!

But it's my only option, thought Zac, carefully pulling the bag over his clothes without letting go of the chopper.

The chopper was coming in to land, dropping lower and lower.

Zac had to time his jump perfectly.

Closer ... a little closer ... nearly ...

Now!

Zac leapt from the helicopter and pulled the ripcord. Instantly, the Super-Ball puffed out into a see-through rubber cage.

It was weirdly quiet inside as Zac plummeted toward the ground.

BOOOOIIIINNNGG!

The Super-Ball bounced on the foot-path and into the air again. Zac flew over the crowds of people shuffling towards the MegArena.

The ball peaked at about a hundred metres in the air, and then dropped back to the ground again. Zac leant against the clear sides of the ball, trying to guide his next bounce.

BOOOOIIIINNNGGG!

A couple more bounces and Zac was close to the MegArena. From way up high, he could see that the stadium's roof was wide open.

If I do another huge bounce, he thought, *I could probably get right inside the stadium.*

As he dropped to the ground again, Zac slammed his weight downwards, forcing the ball to do an even bigger bounce.

BOOOOIIIINNNGGG!

Zac bounced into the stadium's car park and launched up, up, up – and over the side of the MegArena! Zac flew through the open roof, towards the seats below.

Now the disgusting part, he thought. He sucked up as much spit as he could and spat at the wall of the ball.

Straight away, the rubber started oozing and dissolving until …

SPLAT!

Zac and the suit landed in a big gummy mess inside the stadium. Luckily the combination of rubber and saliva provided a soft landing – even if it was gross.

Ewww! thought Zac, sitting up and pulling bits of dissolved rubber out of his hair. *The things I do for GIB.*

Luckily his guitar didn't have too much gunk on it. Zac wiped it clean and looked around. He'd landed in the seats of the MegArena. He could see the stage far below.

If I'm going to figure out how to reverse the mind-control process, I'd better start there, Zac thought, standing up. He looked at the time. It was 4.50 p.m.

Zac could hear the huge crowd outside the stadium. He knew the zombies were all muttering about how great the D-Pod was.

I've got to hurry, he told himself, running to the stage. He climbed up onto it and started looking around for clues.

The instruments were all set up, but it was dark and quiet. Zac walked around, looking for anything out of the ordinary.

Zac thought back to what Drastic had said at the hotel.

He said they kept trying to improve the 'Brain Quake' song, he remembered, *and that the song had to be the way it was to support the Zeta wave …*

Zac wandered over to the drum kit, lost in thought. He sat on the stool, recalling something his granny had once told him.

Then Zac had a brainwave. *What if the key to reversing the mind-control is IN the 'Brain Quake' song?* he thought excitedly. *The first time I heard it, I KNEW it sounded wrong!*

But before Zac could do anything else, he heard a faint click. And then –

KER-**CHUNK!**

A pair of metal bands snapped shut around his waist. The drum kit was booby-trapped!

Then a trap-door opened on the ground in front of him and the drum stool tipped forward.

The metal band around his waist snapped open, dropping Zac underneath the stage!

CHAPTER

Zac fell through the trapdoor into a room full of machines and computer screens. A deep, throbbing noise was coming from somewhere below.

Then suddenly Zac realised he'd *stopped* falling entirely. But he hadn't hit the ground. He was now hanging in mid-air!

What is going on? he wondered, looking around.

Zac was in the air about five metres above the ground, surrounded by giant speakers on all sides. That was where the throbbing noise was coming from. The speakers were playing 'Brain Quake'!

'What do you think of my lovely Boom Box?' someone called from below. 'I've created the world's first cage using soundwaves!'

Zac looked down. 'Dr Drastic!' he said, still suspended in mid-air.

'Please,' Drastic called, his glass eye glinting in the light. 'Call me DJ Draz.'

Zac tried to throw himself out of the way of the sound waves, but he was stuck firm.

He wondered how the soundwaves could hold him up if they weren't even that loud. He made a mental note to ask Leon later.

Rats! he thought. *How am I going to get out of this one?*

'I've tied you up so many times, Agent Rock Star,' Dr Drastic said smugly, 'and you always escape. So I thought I'd try something new.'

Zac watched as Drastic walked over to a wall that was covered in controls. There was a giant slider, like the volume control on a stereo.

The slider was currently on three. At the top was eleven, and at the bottom was a big button marked Mute.

'Level three is loud enough to hold you there,' said Dr Drastic, 'but I might try eleven later, just to see what it does to you.'

If I can push that Mute button, I'll be free, thought Zac, his mind racing.

Then Zac realised something else. Even though 'Brain Quake' was playing, he hadn't turned into a zombie!

'Why haven't you added the Zeta wave to your dumb song?' he asked Drastic.

'I'm not stupid enough to play that down here, Rock Star!' said Dr Drastic. 'It would turn me into my own zombie.'

He waved a hand at his controls.

'Anyway, the best part is that all my D-Pods are linked by wireless data sharing, so I can send my zombies new Zeta waves whenever I like.'

Zac wriggled harder, testing the limits of the soundwaves. But all that happened was the collar of his jacket brushed up against his face, and he got a big glob of Super-Ball rubbery gum in his mouth.

Ew ... It tasted disgusting!

Hang on, the gum! Zac realised, holding the glob in his mouth. Maybe he could use it somehow.

He looked over at the Mute button. *It's a long way away,* he thought, *but it's my only chance.* He needed to keep Dr Drastic talking for just one more minute.

'So what are you going to do with all these zombies?' he asked, trying not to choke on the gum.

'Whatever I want!' cried Dr Drastic. 'Once they're mine forever, I could take over a city. No, a country! No, the world!' He leant over the controls, giggling. 'Hmm, what should I do with my next Zeta wave?'

Zac shrugged his shoulders, trying to move his collar into his mouth. He felt another big gloop of rubbery gum there and managed to get it with his tongue.

That should be enough, thought Zac, gagging.

He aimed carefully, and then hocked the gum as hard as he could.

The gum sailed across the room, right in the direction of the Mute button.

SPLATTT!

The gum smacked into the button, and the song cut out instantly. The soundwaves released Zac and he dropped to the floor with an expert roll.

Dr Drastic spun around. 'Agent Rock Star!' he cried.

Zac raced over to the big pile of D-Pods and grabbed one. Before Drastic had time to react, Zac shoved the earphones in his ears!

The D-Pod had an instant effect.

Drastic stood there limply, staring at the ground. 'These D-Pods are totally awesome,' he mumbled. 'Must wear my lovely D-Pod.'

He won't be controlling anyone for a while, thought Zac. *He's become his own zombie!*

CHAPTER 10

Zac had caught Dr Drastic, but it was now 5.47 p.m. There were only 12 minutes until the concert started!

All the zombies would be gathering up in the MegArena, moments away from becoming permanent zombies.

Zac gulped. *Think!* he told himself. *What could reverse the mind-control process?*

Reverse ...

Zac had always thought 'Brain Quake' had its notes out of order. And Ricky Blazes had said it would sound better backwards.

I bet that's it!

There was only enough time to try one thing. Zac hoped desperately that his hunch was right. Otherwise the zombies would be zombies forever.

Zac grabbed his guitar, which was still slung over his back. He ran to the big main door of the lab, but it wouldn't open.

There's no time for me to pick the lock, he thought. *I need to find another way back to the stage.*

He looked up. High above, the trapdoor

he'd fallen through still hung open.

How do I get up there? thought Zac.

His backpack was empty. The Boom Box speakers were too spongy to use his sneakers on. His SHADES and guitar were no good for climbing. All he had left was the cool leather jacket from the CamoSine.

It looked like a normal leather jacket. But since when was anything from GIB normal?

Zac looked closely at it. There were tiny labels sewn all over it that said things like 'laser blow-torch' and 'anti-piranha spray'.

This wasn't a normal jacket. It was a GIB Escape Jacket!

Zac pressed the label marked 'jet packs'.

He grinned as two slim rockets unfolded on his back. Then ...

VRRROOOOOMMM!

Zac zoomed up through the trapdoor. He pressed the label again and the jets cut out, plonking him nicely on stage.

The MegArena was now completely full, and Zac's SHADES told him that 90% were D-Pod zombies. But no-one was mumbling anymore.

It was eerily quiet in the huge stadium. Everything was dark ... except for a single spotlight at the front of the stage.

Zac had only minutes left.

He walked into the spotlight and swung his electric guitar around, setting it to AutoAmplify. Then Zac took a deep breath and started playing. He started from the end of 'Brain Quake', playing the song entirely in reverse.

At first it was hard to remember the notes, like saying the alphabet backwards. But once he got going, it sounded pretty good.

This isn't a bad song, he thought. *Let's really make it rock!*

He turned the dials on his guitar way up to maximum.

BLAM! ZANG! TWANG!

Zac saw a few of the zombies down the front take off their D-Pods and shake their heads.

It was working! More and more zombies were waking up. Some of them started cheering for Zac. He ran up and down the stage, playing as hard and fast as he could.

TWANNG! SLAMMM!

The cheering was getting louder, and some people started dancing.

Then Zac saw the members of Axe Grinder climbing up on stage. They gave him a smile, grabbed their instruments and joined in!

Soon the whole crowd was jumping and cheering.

He'd done it! Everyone was safe! Zac and Axe Grinder hammered down the last notes of the song. A hundred thousand new Tom Rocket fans went wild.

'Nice work, Tom Rocket!' yelled Ricky Blazes. 'Next song is "Rock Your World". You ready?'

Zac was about to say 'You bet!' when a message popped up on his SHADES.

Great work on the mission, Zac!
Now, what did you get Mum
for her birthday?
From Agent Tool Belt (Dad) x

ZAC POWER

SWAMP RACE

CHAPTER

Zac Power pulled another shirt out of the washing basket. He was not having a good night.

Zac's parents had been called into his school for a meeting. The principal had noticed that Zac had missed a lot of school lately, and she wanted to know why.

The truth was that Zac was a highly

trained secret agent for the Government Investigation Bureau (GIB for short). He had to keep skipping class to go on dangerous spy missions.

But the principal wasn't allowed to know that. It was all top secret. As far she knew, Zac was just a normal kid. Zac's parents would have to come up with a good story to explain why he kept disappearing. Zac's parents and his brother Leon were all spies, too.

As if that whole mess at school wasn't bad enough, Zac's mum had left him at home with a massive load of washing to fold. Zac had been slaving away for ages already and he was only halfway through the huge basket of clothes. He reached down again and pulled out a pair of Leon's underpants.

'Ugh!' he groaned. 'Gross!'

The worst bit was that Zac's parents had decided he needed a babysitter while they were out. Usually, Zac would be left with Leon at times like this. But Zac's geeky older brother was out tonight, too.

Which meant that Zac was stuck at home with some random babysitter. And all night she'd done nothing but watch TV and talk on her phone.

It's so unfair! Zac grumbled to himself. *I've been to the MOON and back by myself, but I'm not allowed to stay home alone for a few hours? It doesn't make any sense!*

Zac decided to take a break from folding the washing. He pulled out his SpyPad (the high-powered tablet carried by every GIB agent) and began checking his SpyMail.

A sudden voice behind Zac made him jump. The babysitter was coming down the hall towards him, still talking into her phone.

'Yeah, OK,' she was saying. 'I'll give it to him now.'

Zac quickly stashed his SpyPad into the washing basket, hiding it from view just as the babysitter walked into the room.

'Hi, Zac,' she said.

'What do you want?' said Zac grumpily.

'Don't be so cranky,' said the babysitter, smiling. 'I've got something for you.'

Yeah, right, thought Zac. *What could you possibly have that I'd want?*

But Zac's mouth dropped open as he saw what was in the babysitter's hand. It was a shiny silver disk. A mission from GIB.

Zac stared at the girl. Obviously this was no ordinary babysitter!

The babysitter flashed a GIB card. 'Agent Blizzard at your service,' she said. 'Go on, you'd better read the mission.'

Zac pulled his SpyPad out of the washing basket and stuck the disk inside.

'You'd better get going,' said Agent Blizzard. 'Your brother is waiting across

CLASSIFIED

MISSION INITIATED: 6 P.M.
CURRENT TIME: 8.23 P.M.

GIB has received a message from the enemy agent Professor Voler.

Voler has the blueprints for a high-tech spying device called the X-Beam.

Voler says he is willing to give these blueprints away. He has invited you to a meeting on his jet to discuss this matter.

His offer expires at 6:00pm tomorrow.

YOUR MISSION
Meet with Professor Voler and retrieve the X-Beam blueprints.

END

the road to brief you.'

Zac nodded and ran for the door. *Well,* he thought, *looks like I'll be missing another day of school tomorrow.*

CHAPTER

Zac raced outside and looked around for Leon. He spotted a big laundry service van parked on the other side of the street.

Zac knew that this was no ordinary van. It was the Mobile Technology Lab, Leon's disguised laboratory on wheels. Zac slid open the van door and climbed in. Inside the MTL, Leon was busy tinkering at a workbench. Tinkering was what Leon did best. He was a GIB technical officer, in charge of developing gadgets and organising missions.

'There you are!' said Leon, turning around. 'Time to get moving. You have to be at the drop-off point by 6.30 a.m.'

Leon pushed a button and the MTL started rumbling along the road. Zac noticed that it was driving on autopilot.

'Where's the drop-off point?' Zac asked, glancing at the time on his SpyPad.

8.30 P.M.

'Professor Voler wants us to leave you at a place out in the bush,' said Leon. 'He'll pick you up from there.'

'Why?'

'You know what Voler's like,' Leon said. 'Everything has to be totally secret. He wants to be sure you're alone before you get on his jet.'

Zac nodded. Professor Voler was a strange old thief who lived in an enormous jet. He spent most of his time flying around stealing rare technology.

Zac had met Voler once before, but the old man had escaped before Zac could arrest him.

'So why is Voler giving away this free technology?' Zac asked. 'It sounds like a trap to me.'

'I know,' said Leon. 'We think so, too.

But it's worth the risk if you can get your hands on those X-Beam blueprints.'

'What is an X-Beam, anyway?' Zac asked.

'It's kind of like an X-ray,' said Leon. 'But instead of looking through skin and bone, it lets you see through solid brick and metal. In theory, that is.'

'What do you mean, *in theory?*' said Zac, raising his eyebrows.

'Well,' said Leon, 'that's what an X-Beam is *supposed* to do, but no-one's ever come up with working blueprints before.'

'Until now,' said Zac.

Leon nodded. 'Which is why we need to make sure Voler's blueprints don't fall into the wrong hands. Imagine what would happen if BIG got hold of them!'

BIG were the most ruthless spies in the business and GIB's greatest enemies. It would be a disaster if BIG could make a working X-Beam!

'So, what's the plan for this mission?' Zac asked, leaning on the workbench and glancing out the front window. The MTL was travelling along the open highway now.

'Well, obviously we're not going to send you out there unprotected,' said Leon, picking up what looked like a metal T-shirt. 'This is Electro-Armour, the latest in GIB personal safety gear. It should shield you from just about anything Voler can throw at you.'

'Excellent,' said Zac, grabbing the armour.

'That panel on the front is electrically charged,' said Leon, pointing at the chest. 'It'll zap anything that touches it.'

Zac pulled off his shirt and carefully slipped on the Electro-Armour. While he did that, Leon turned to his bench and pushed a few buttons.

'So that's the plan?' Zac said, putting his shirt back on over the top. 'I just head out to the bush wearing a metal T-shirt, figure out how to get hold of the blueprints and – *whoa!*'

Zac was nearly thrown off his feet. For a moment he thought he had electrocuted himself with the Electro-Armour. But then he realised that the MTL had suddenly started hurtling forward, tearing down the highway at incredible speeds.

'Leon!' Zac shouted, steadying himself. 'What's going on?'

'I've added a few upgrades to the MTL,' said Leon. 'Ready for take-off?'

Zac stared at Leon. 'Ready for *what*?'

Leon just grinned at him.

Zac grabbed hold of the workbench at the front of the truck and stared out the window. Huge flat wings were unfolding from underneath the MTL.

A second later, the van lifted off the ground and soared up into the dark night sky.

'Well?' said Leon, smirking. 'What do you think?'

'It's awesome,' said Zac. 'But if you do something like that again without warning me, I'm going to switch on my Electro-Armour and give you a big hug.'

CHAPTER 3

'How much further?' Zac asked, yawning. He stretched and sat up in his seat.

The Mobile Technology Lab had been flying all night, and Zac could just see the sun starting to rise in the distance.

'Almost there,' said Leon. 'We're coming up to the drop-off point now.'

A few minutes later, Leon landed the

MTL at the edge of some bushland. 'See that big rock over there?' he said, pointing. 'That's where you're supposed to wait. You'd better hurry, too. It's almost time.'

Zac nodded and climbed out of the van. As he watched, the MTL rumbled across the grass and took off into the air again.

Zac walked through the bush and stopped at the rock where Leon had told him to wait. He checked the time.

6.31 A.M.

Voler had said to be here at 6.30 a.m. but so far Zac couldn't see any sign of –

CRASH!

Zac's eyes darted upwards. Something big and heavy was crashing down through the trees above his head. Zac leapt out of the way just in time.

THUD!

A big wooden crate hit the ground — right where Zac had been standing!

Zac walked over and looked at the crate. Then he stared up at the sky. Zac knew Professor Voler's jet was protected by advanced cloaking technology. It was obviously hovering somewhere above him, but Zac couldn't see it.

Am I supposed to open the crate? wondered Zac. *It's been nailed shut!*

CRASH!

Something else was coming down through the trees.

Zac took cover again.

CLANK!

A big metal crowbar landed neatly on top of the crate.

Right, thought Zac. He jammed the crowbar into the crate and levered off the lid. Inside was what looked like a heavy black wetsuit.

Sitting on top of the suit was a handwritten note.

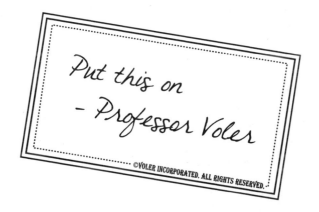

Put this on
– Professor Voler

Zac pulled the suit on over his clothes. A metal rectangle, the size of a shoebox, bulged out the back of the suit.

On the sleeve of the suit, Zac noticed a tiny control stick and a row of buttons. He tapped at the controls but nothing happened.

Maybe the suit got damaged in the fall, he thought. But then the box on Zac's back started jolting wildly. He staggered forward. *What on earth —?*

Three long metal blades were unfolding out of the box. The blades flattened above Zac's head, and then started spinning around and around like the ones on a helicopter.

'Whoa!'

Suddenly, Zac lifted off the ground. The helicopter blades sent leaves flying as he rose up between the trees.

Zac jiggled the control stick but it was no good. Someone was steering his Chopper Suit and it wasn't him.

Voler must have this thing hooked up to a remote control, thought Zac.

The Chopper Suit flew up through the air, guided by its invisible pilot. Zac was jolted across to the left, then straight up, then to the right again. Then he stopped, hovering on the spot.

Zac peered around for some sign of Voler's cloaked jet. He could hear the rumbling of a big engine, but he couldn't see anything.

HISSSS-CLUNK!

A hatch suddenly opened up in the empty sky above Zac.

A-ha! Zac thought. *This must be it.*

As the metal door hissed open, the jet's cloak flickered slightly. Zac caught a glimpse of the huge flying machine floating above him.

The Chopper Suit started moving again and Zac was lifted up through the hatch, into the jet.

HISSSS-CLUNK!

The hatch hissed shut beneath Zac's feet. With one final jolt of the Chopper

Suit, he touched down inside the jet.

There was a big round button on the chest of Zac's suit marked 'REMOVE'. Zac pushed it.

SNAP!

The Chopper Suit popped right off his body and landed in a heap on the floor.

Zac looked around him. He was in a big round room filled with jet-packs, parachutes, and other kinds of personal flying machines.

There was a ladder leading up out of the room. Zac climbed up and found himself inside a narrow hallway.

Zac walked down and opened the door at the end. He stepped into an enormous lounge room. It was filled with beautiful antique furniture and decorated with priceless paintings and statues. All around the walls were shelves stuffed with hundreds of stolen artefacts and gadgets.

'Ah,' said a voice. 'Zachary! You're just in time for breakfast.'

Zac turned and saw Professor Voler sitting at his ornate wooden tea table, dressed in his usual suit and tie. He was buttering some toast and smiling warmly at Zac.

Then Zac saw something that made his stomach turn. Voler wasn't alone.

Sitting in a chair opposite the professor was BIG agent Caz Rewop.

CHAPTER

'Caz!' Zac snarled.

12-year-old Caz Rewop was one of BIG's most dangerous spies. Zac had met her several times before. He knew she was nothing but trouble.

Caz didn't look too happy to see Zac either. 'Agent Rock Star,' she growled, leaping to her feet.

She was carrying a big stick with a BIG logo stamped onto the handle. Caz gave it a flick, and a bright red cord of electricity shot out the end. She held the gadget like a whip towards Zac, ready to strike.

Zac looked from Caz to Voler and back again. *WHAT is going on?*

'What's *he* doing here?' Caz demanded, glaring at Voler.

'Me?' said Zac. 'Why are *you* here?'

'Everyone, please, settle down,' said Voler, standing up calmly. 'If you'll kindly take your seats, I will explain everything.'

Zac and Caz didn't move. They just stood there, frozen on the spot, glaring at each other.

'Come now,' smiled Voler. 'Your breakfast is getting cold.'

He pulled the cover off a tray piled
high with bacon, eggs, sausages and hash
browns.

Zac sat down at the table, shaking his
head.

He knew Voler was nothing but a thief
and a liar, and he didn't trust the old man's
kindness for a second. But co-operating
with Voler seemed like his best chance of
getting the X-Beam blueprints.

Caz seemed to agree. She gave Zac one
last glare, then switched off her Electro-
magnetic Whip and took her seat again.

'There we are,' said Voler cheerfully,

beginning to serve out the breakfast. 'Now, I suppose you're both wondering about those X-Beam blueprints.'

'What do the blueprints have to do with *him?*' said Caz angrily, stabbing a finger in Zac's direction. 'You said you were going to give them to BIG!'

'What?' said Zac, his eyes darting over to Professor Voler. 'You said you were giving them to GIB!'

'Actually,' Voler corrected, 'what I *said* was that I am willing to give the blueprints away. I never said to *whom*.'

Voler put a plate of food down in front of each of them. Then he reached into his pocket and pulled out a small plastic toad.

'Inside this plastic toad is a Data Storage Device, or a DSD, which contains everything you need to build a working X-Beam,' Voler explained.

'And how do we get it?' Zac asked.

'I propose a competition,' said Voler, picking up a silver knife and fork. 'In a few hours, the two of you will be dropped off in the Murky Swamp. This DSD will be hiding somewhere down there. Whoever finds it first may keep it.'

'That's it?' said Caz suspiciously.

Voler nodded. 'That's it.'

'But why?' asked Zac. 'Why are you doing this? You've spent your whole life stealing things from other people! Why are you suddenly giving stuff away?'

'Those blueprints mean nothing to me,' said Voler with a wave of his hand. 'Look around you. I have all the riches I need. What I want now is to be *entertained*.'

'Entertained?' said Zac. 'You mean this whole thing is just some twisted game for your amusement?'

'Yes and no,' said Voler. 'I shall certainly enjoy watching you compete. But I assure you this is far more than just a game.'

He took a sip from his tea cup and then continued.

'There are dangerous things in that swamp, Zachary. Toxic waters. Creatures that are big enough to swallow you whole.

Not to mention a few of my own little surprises.'

'And what if I refuse?' demanded Caz. 'What if I don't want to play your game?'

'Then Zachary gets the DSD all to himself,' said Voler. 'Of course, if it is Zachary who refuses, the DSD is yours.'

Zac stared at Voler. There was no way he was letting Caz get her hands on those blueprints. And from the look in her eyes, Caz was thinking the same thing.

'I'm in,' she said.

'Me too,' said Zac.

'Excellent,' said Voler, clasping his hands together. 'We begin in three hours.'

Zac glanced at his watch.

6.57 A.M.

Voler smiled again and picked up his knife and fork.

'Now then,' he said brightly, 'time to eat this breakfast! You've got a big day ahead of you and you're going to need all the energy you can get.'

CHAPTER 5

'Here are the rules,' said Voler, pacing up and down in front of Zac and Caz.

They had finished breakfast, and now Voler's jet was hovering just above the Murky Swamp. Zac, Caz and Voler were down in the room full of flying machines, where Zac had first arrived.

'Rule number one,' said Voler. 'You may

go anywhere in the swamp and the forest.'

Zac nodded.

'Rule number two,' Voler continued. 'You are only allowed to take the equipment you were carrying when you arrived.'

Caz held up her Electromagnetic Whip and grinned nastily at Zac.

Zac felt around in his pocket for the SpyPad. *Lucky for me this thing is about a hundred gadgets in one,* he thought.

'Rule number three,' said Voler. 'You have until 6 p.m. to find the blueprints.'

Zac looked at the time.

9.59 A.M.

'What happens if neither of us has found the blueprints by then?' Zac asked.

'Then I will leave the pair of you behind and be on my way,' said Voler. 'And believe me when I say that you do *not* want to be stranded in the Murky Swamp after dark.'

Voler reached into his suit pocket. He pulled out two yellow envelopes and handed one each to Zac and Caz.

'Open these when you get down to the swamp,' Voler instructed. 'The clues inside will help you find the blueprints. I have also scattered a few other vehicles and so on around the swamp for you to uncover. You are allowed to use whatever you find.'

Voler pulled two green parachutes – or things that looked like parachutes – down from hooks on the wall. Each one was made from a big sheet of flexible plastic, stretched over a metal frame. The frames arched up in the middle, pulling the plastic into a dome shape.

'Put these on,' said Voler..

Zac took his parachute and strapped himself into the harness. Caz did the same.

'Excellent,' said Voler. 'Well, good luck!' He reached over and pulled a lever on the wall.

'Wait!' said Zac. 'What if –?'

HISSSS-CLUNK!

But then the metal trapdoor clanked open under Zac's feet and he was falling through the air. He reached up and firmly gripped the parachute cables.

FWOOMP!

The parachute filled up with air, slowing his fall.

Twisting his body left and right, Zac found that he could steer the parachute in any direction. He began gliding down towards the swamp in wide, lazy circles.

The flexible metal harness responded to his tiniest movements. It was almost like the parachute was part of his body.

This is incredible! thought Zac. *Why hasn't Leon come up with a design like this?*

There was a sudden flash of movement in front of Zac. Caz was speeding towards him on a collision course. She was trying to knock him out of the sky!

WHOOSH!

At the last second, Zac swooped clear of Caz's path. Caz went spinning through the air, only just managing to keep control of her parachute.

Trust Caz to play dirty, Zac thought to himself. He tilted his body forward, increasing his speed. He dived down towards the swamp, then pulled up at the last second and...

SPLASH!

He hit the muddy water feet-first and quickly began pulling off his parachute harness.

Moments later, Zac saw Caz splash down a few metres away.

Standing waist-deep in the water, Zac took Voler's envelope out of his pocket. He tore it open and pulled out three soggy cards with shapes printed on them.

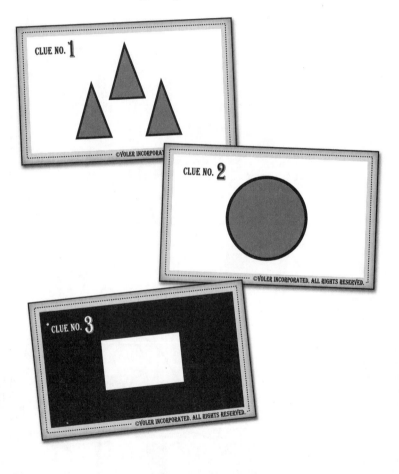

Great, thought Zac. *What on earth are these?*

He looked around at the swamp he had landed in. Dirty brown water stretched out in all directions. Here and there, little islands of mud rose up from the water.

Up ahead, way off in the distance, Zac could see a forest. And to his left, two enormous mountains stretched towards the sky.

Mountains! thought Zac, staring down at the first card. *Is that what these triangles are supposed to be?*

Caz seemed to think so. Looking around, Zac saw her splashing through the water in the direction of the mountains.

'I'll wait for you at the finish line, Agent Rock Star!' she called over her shoulder.

Zac was about to follow her when he noticed something. *Hold on*, he thought. *Why are there three triangles on the card and only TWO mountains?*

He peered around the swamp again. Maybe that wasn't the answer after all.

Then the forest in the distance caught Zac's eye again. What if those triangles on the card were meant to be trees?

Zac decided to follow his hunch.

He turned away from Caz and sprinted off in the direction of the forest.

CHAPTER

Hours later, Zac was still wading through the swamp in the direction of the trees.

He was almost there, but it was hard going. The hot sun beat down on him. There were spiky reeds growing everywhere. The mud at the bottom of the swamp grabbed at his feet with every step.

Zac was starting to wonder whether

he'd made the right choice after all.

SPLASH!

Zac whirled around, but there was nothing there. Just ripples on the water.

He was sure he'd heard something moving behind him. *Probably just a tree branch falling into the swamp,* he told himself. *Just concentrate on finding the blueprints.*

But then Zac felt something slither past his leg. Something big.

OK, he thought, *I definitely didn't imagine that.*

Zac started moving more quickly through the water, trying to get away from whatever was swimming around down there.

SPLASH!

'Aaahh!'

Something long and grey leapt up into the air in front of Zac, then splashed back down into the water.

An eel! Zac realised with a shudder.

But this was no ordinary eel. It was as thick as a tree trunk, with big pointed teeth. How was that even possible?

There must be something in the water, Zac thought. *Something toxic that makes the animals get like that.*

But he decided to leave the scientific explanations to Leon and concentrate on not getting eaten.

Up ahead, there was a huge fallen tree

poking out of the water. Zac waded over and pulled himself up on top of it.

Looking down, he saw the eel circling the tree, getting ready to leap up and attack again. *Eels are so gross,* he thought to himself, getting out his SpyPad.

He set it to Laser and pointed the SpyPad down at the water. Then he adjusted the beam setting to Maximum Power.

At first, the eel didn't seem to react. It just kept on swimming in circles around Zac. But then the water started to steam and bubble, boiling in the heat of the laser.

The eel leapt out of the water again. It let out an ear-splitting screech and snapped its jaws at Zac.

Zac ducked out of the way just in time, grabbing hold of a branch to steady himself.

SPLASH!

The horrible creature crashed down into the swamp and slithered away.

Zac let out a long sigh and waited for the water around him to cool down again. He scanned the area with his SpyPad.

No sign of Caz or the DSD.

Then Zac noticed something that made his eyes light up. It was one of the little mud islands that dotted the swamp. Most of these islands had only a few little bushes or weeds growing on them.

But this one was different. There were three trees sitting on top of it.

Zac pulled Voler's cards out of his pocket and glanced at the picture of the three triangles.

This must be it!

Zac dived down into the water and hurried across to the mud island. He climbed up between the trees and looked around for some clue about what to do next.

'If these trees are the triangles,' Zac said, thinking out loud, 'then the next thing I need to find is something round.'

PEOOWW!

Great, thought Zac. *Now what?*

His eyes flashed to the sky. Hovering through the air towards him was what looked like a black metal soccer ball.

Well, I guess that would be the round thing I'm supposed to be looking for.

Unfortunately, this particular round thing also happened to be firing lasers straight at him.

Zac crouched down behind one of the trees.

Zac had seen Voler use a weapon a bit like this before, the first time they had met. He knew that it had motion sensors which triggered the laser blasts. It was called a Laser Orb.

PEOOWW!

Another blast from the Laser Orb shattered the tree into splinters.

Don't move, Zac reminded himself. *If I don't move, it can't see me.*

Zac froze on the spot, his fingers digging into a pile of sticky mud on the ground. The Laser Orb hovered closer to him.

It spun around slowly, looking for any sign of movement.

Closer, closer...

Suddenly, Zac leapt up into the air and threw a massive glob of mud at the Orb's motion sensors.

SPLAT!

The Orb shuddered in mid-air, then hovered quietly on the spot.

Zac stood up slowly, making sure the motion sensors really were disabled.

But the mud had stuck and was now drying over the Orb.

'Congratulations, Zachary,' said a familiar voice. It was Voler. His voice was coming from a speaker inside the Orb.

CLUNK! CLUNK!

Two small handles had suddenly appeared from underneath the Orb.

'Well?' said Voler's voice. 'What are you waiting for?'

Zac stared at the Orb floating above his head. Then he leapt into the air, grabbing hold of the handles.

Shuddering slightly under Zac's weight, the Orb lifted him into the air and zoomed away across the swamp.

CHAPTER 7

For the second time that day, Zac found himself soaring high above the Murky Swamp. Voler's Laser Orb was surprisingly fast, and not easy to hold onto. Zac's arms quickly got tired, and a couple of times he almost lost his grip.

The Orb zoomed through the air, guiding Zac past more and more of the same endless swamp. But there was still no sign of the plastic toad with the DSD inside.

This place is massive, thought Zac. *Those blueprints could be anywhere!*

VROOOOOM!

Zac looked back over his shoulder. Caz was beneath him, sitting aboard a shiny orange hovercraft!

That must be one of the vehicles that Voler left for us to find, Zac realised.

The hovercraft tore across the swamp, bucking and bouncing, sending an enormous spray of water out behind it.

Caz looked up and saw Zac hovering above her. She shot him a look of pure hatred. But she seemed to decide that Zac was heading in the right direction. Caz brought the hovercraft around, ready to chase after Zac.

But Zac was moving too quickly for her. The Laser Orb kept on pulling him through the air, and before long Caz was just a speck in the distance.

Still clinging to the Orb, Zac craned his neck to look up at his watch.

In just over three hours, Voler's jet would fly away and Zac would be stranded in the swamp. And who knew where this flying ball was taking him? Zac began to wonder whether he should just let go of the Orb and continue his search back on the ground.

But the Orb had other ideas.

WHOOOOOSH!

Suddenly, the Laser Orb took a sharp turn to the right. Zac's left hand slipped off the Orb and he had to scramble to get his grip back.

Now Zac could see the end of the swamp coming into view below him. Tall trees grew up from the mud like a green wall, all along the water's edge. With a jolt, Zac felt the Orb begin flying downwards. It was coming in to land.

Zac flew lower and lower, until his feet were almost touching the surface of the water. The Orb reached the swamp's edge and came to a stop between two trees.

I guess I'm here, thought Zac, dropping to the ground. *Wherever 'here' is.*

As soon as Zac let go of the Orb, it whizzed up into the sky and flew away.

Zac pulled out Voler's clues again. The last card was all dark except for a white rectangle. He started walking through the trees, looking for anything that might be a good match.

Walking deeper into the forest, Zac saw a shape that looked darker than the trees around it. He walked over for a closer look. It was the entrance to a big stony cave. Zac's spy senses tingled.

He switched on his SpyPad's torch and stepped inside.

Zac's torch wasn't the only light in the cave. Further inside the cave, something else was glowing.

Zac headed in the direction of the light. *Is there someone else in here?* he wondered. Surely there was no way Caz could have overtaken him!

Zac rounded a corner and finally found the source of the light. It was an enormous computer screen showing a map of the Murky Swamp.

Ah, Zac thought to himself. *The screen must be the white square on the clue card.*

The map on the screen was black and white – except for one little island that was glowing bright red.

That must be where the X-Beam blueprints are hidden! Zac realised. He quickly pulled out his SpyPad and carefully snapped a photo of the map. But then a sudden noise from outside broke his concentration.

Back out in the swamp, someone had just let out a terrified, ear-splitting scream.

CHAPTER

Zac raced out of the cave and back towards the swamp. He reached the edge of the water and saw right away who had been screaming.

It was Caz. She was standing aboard her little hovercraft, cracking her Electro-magnetic Whip at a massive crocodile.

Caz brought the whip down again

and again, sending sparks flying. But the crocodile didn't even seem to notice that it was being hit.

The hovercraft rocked back and forth, and Zac could see that it was only a matter of time before the croc knocked Caz right into the water.

Zac sighed. He knew what he had to do.

He jumped back into the swamp and began wading out. *Towards* the crocodile.

But as he got closer, he realised that it wasn't a real crocodile at all. Instead of scales, the croc was covered in grey steel plating. Instead of eyes, two red lights blinked menacingly in Caz's direction.

It was a robotic crocodile! It must have

been planted there by Professor Voler.

As if the real animals in this place aren't bad enough! thought Zac, remembering the eel.

He crept up behind the robocodile, trying to keep from being seen. Zac remembered something he'd seen on Leon's favourite nature show, *Creepy Creatures*.

Zac leapt up onto the robocodile's back, just as it took another lunge at Caz.

CLANK!

The robocodile's mouth snapped shut. Zac grabbed onto the closed jaws and held on tight.

For a second he thought his plan had

worked. But then the robocodile snapped its mouth open again, flipped Zac over and threw him into the swamp.

SPLASH!

I guess that rule only works for real crocodiles, thought Zac, getting to his feet. He decided to switch on his Electro-Armour just to be safe.

Caz cowered on the hovercraft, but the robocodile had already started swimming towards Zac.

Zac turned and ran through the shallow water, but his feet kept slipping into the mud, slowing him down. In seconds, the robocodile was right on top of him. It stretched its mouth wide. Looking up,

Zac saw row after row of razor-sharp steel teeth.

Uh-oh, he thought, trying to dart out of the way. But the robocodile lunged right for him. Its mechanical jaws came down on top of Zac, right across his chest.

CLANK!

Luckily, Zac's arms were up in the air, and the robocodile's metal teeth crunched down hard on his Electro-Armour.

KZZZZZK-POW!

The armour sent a surge of electricity into the robocodile's mouth. The croc shot up into the air, twisting and sparking. Zac could see that its systems had been fried instantly.

SPLASH!

Zac dived out of the way as the roboc-odile came crashing into the water, completely destroyed.

Zac stood up and paddled over to Caz's hovercraft.

'I thought you were done for,' said Caz, sounding almost disappointed that the croc hadn't finished him off. 'He bit you straight across the chest! How'd you survive that?'

Zac lifted up his shirt to reveal the Electro-Armour hiding underneath.

'Hey!' Caz protested. 'How come you've got *armour?*'

'I wouldn't be complaining if I were

you,' said Zac. 'This armour just saved your life!'

'Well, I'm fine now,' said Caz, crossing her arms. 'So you can get out of here.'

But when Zac looked down and saw the time, he knew it wasn't going to be that simple.

4.01 P.M.

There were only two hours left! He cringed as he realised what he was going to have to do next.

'Well?' said Caz. 'What are you waiting for? Get lost!'

'No,' said Zac. 'Let me onto that hovercraft.'

'Yeah, right,' Caz laughed.

'I know where the plastic toad is hidden,' said Zac. 'But we're going to have to go together.'

'I'm not going anywhere with you, Rock Star,' Caz growled.

'You think *I* want to be stuck with *you*?' said Zac. 'In two hours, Voler's going to fly off and leave us both behind. You can't even stay alive in the *daytime* without my help. Do you really want to be stuck here at night?'

'No-one *asked* you to help me,' Caz spat. 'I had it all under control.'

'Really?' said Zac, raising an eyebrow.

Caz glared at Zac, but was silent.

'Look,' Zac said, trying to keep calm.

'You've got the hovercraft, but no idea where the plastic toad is. I've got a map to the plastic toad but no way to get there. The only way we can get out of here is if we work together.'

Caz stared at him, weighing up her options. Then she let out a groan of disgust.

'Fine,' she said. 'Get on.'

CHAPTER 9

The hovercraft tore across the surface of the swamp, towards the island where the X-Beam blueprints were hidden.

VROOOOOM!

Even though it was Zac who knew the way to the island, Caz had refused to let him drive. So Zac sat looking over Caz's shoulder, shouting directions over the roar of the engine. He kept his SpyPad hidden in his pocket, and only checked the map when he was sure Caz wasn't looking.

Apart from that, they kept silent.

They may have been working together now, but they both knew that their agreement would be over as soon as they stepped off the hovercraft.

Even now, sitting behind Caz, Zac was half-tempted to shove her overboard and drive off without her. But he sighed instead and checked the time.

5.32 P.M.

'Right!' he shouted to Caz. 'No, wait — turn left!'

Everything looked so different from the

ground. It was hard to figure out which way they were supposed to be going.

But then he saw it. Up ahead was an island of mud with two big trees knocked down and arranged into the shape of an X.

X marks the spot, thought Zac. This had to be it.

'Over there!' he called.

Caz guided the hovercraft over to the island and brought it to a stop.

Zac stood up and reached for his SpyPad, ready to check the map one last time.

CRACK!

Caz lashed Zac across the back with her whip. Zac's Electro-Armour sparked and kept him from getting hurt, but the impact was enough to send him staggering overboard.

SPLASH!

Zac got to his feet and clambered up onto the island, right behind Caz.

Caz raced around the island, searching frantically for Voler's plastic toad.

Zac, meanwhile, headed straight for the centre of the X-shape made by the fallen trees. He found a patch of long, brown grass and started digging through it.

His hand caught on something that was sticking up out of the ground. Brushing the grass aside, Zac saw that it was a rusty metal lever. He took a deep breath and pulled.

THUD!

Caz ran over and shoved Zac aside, knocking him to the ground. She grabbed the lever for herself and started heaving at it with all her might.

Zac scrambled to his feet and tried to pry Caz's hands off the handle.

'Get off, Rock Star!' growled Caz. 'Those blueprints are *mine.*'

Both of them were holding onto the handle now, trying to shove each other away and pull on the lever at the same time.

Slowly the lever started to shift. *CREEEAAK!*

They dragged it up and over, until it was pointing away in the opposite direction.

For a moment, nothing happened.

Zac and Caz let go of the lever and stepped apart from each other.

Then, a few metres away, the swamp started to bubble and churn. A strange clattering sound came up from under the water. Then something big and round started rising slowly up out of the swamp.

At first, the thing was so covered in mud that they couldn't see what it was. But then the mud started dripping back down into the swamp, revealing a big glass dome.

Inside the dome, sitting on top of a stone platform, was a neatly folded Chopper Suit. It was just like the one that Zac had used to board Voler's jet that morning.

Walking to the edge of the island for

a closer look, Zac noticed something else sitting on the platform.

It was a small plastic toad. The blueprints must be hidden inside!

Zac glanced at Caz. She had seen it, too.

But before either of them could react, they were distracted by another sound.

WHOOMF-WHOOMF!

Someone was coming down out of the sky towards them, wearing a Chopper Suit. It was Professor Voler.

Voler touched down on the island and looked from Zac to Caz.

'Well, well,' he said with a grin. 'A GIB agent and a BIG agent working together! I never thought I'd see the day.'

CHAPTER 10

'Working together?' Caz laughed. 'I was only using him to get to the blueprints!'

Zac's eyes were fixed on Voler. The professor tapped at the controls on his sleeve, and the helicopter blades folded back into his Chopper Suit.

'Please don't let me interrupt,' said Voler, grinning at the two of them. 'I just thought I'd come down here for a closer view of the big finish.'

CREEEAAK!

Zac's eyes flashed across to the dome in the swamp. The glass was splitting apart. He leapt into the water and splashed towards the dome, with Caz right behind him.

Zac and Caz reached the dome at the same time and dived for the plastic toad. They crashed down onto the platform, hands grabbing wildly.

Zac felt his fingers close around the toad. *Yes!*

SPLASH!

Caz barrelled into Zac and they tumbled into the water. Zac wriggled free of her and made his way back up onto the island.

He slipped the plastic toad into his pocket, right next to his SpyPad. Looking back over his shoulder, he saw Caz climbing up out of the water.

Then Zac realised his mistake. He may have got his hands on the plastic toad, but Caz had taken the spare Chopper Suit.

'Well now, this *is* an interesting twist!' said Voler, smiling at Zac. 'You've tracked down my X-Beam blueprints, but now you've got no way of escaping the swamp.'

Voler turned to Caz.

'And *you've* got the Chopper Suit, but no blueprints,' he said. 'How do you suppose you're going to –?'

CRACK!

In a flash, Caz had switched on her Electromagnetic Whip and cracked it at Voler. The cord of electricity struck the big round 'REMOVE' button on the chest of his Chopper Suit.

SNAP!

The Chopper Suit popped right off Voler and landed in a crumpled heap in the grass. Caz reached down and grabbed the suit before Voler had time to react.

'Wait!' said Voler, looking furious. 'You can't do that! It's not in the rules!'

'It is now,' sneered Caz.

Voler shot Caz a dangerous look. But Caz waved her whip at him and he backed off. Then she walked across to Zac, carrying the two Chopper Suits.

'Here's the deal,' she said. 'You hand over the toad and I give you one of these suits.'

Zac looked across at Voler, who was staring angrily at them. Zac had just remembered something and he was sure Caz wouldn't like it!

Fighting the urge to grin, he looked back at Caz and sighed loudly.

'I guess giving up the plastic toad is the only way I'm going to get out of here,' he said, shrugging. 'OK, it's a deal.'

He pulled the toad from his pocket and handed it to Caz. Then he grabbed one of her Chopper Suits and put it on.

'I hope you two have learnt a lesson today,' said Caz, slipping into her own Chopper Suit and backing away from them. *'Don't mess with BIG!'*

She tapped at the suit's controls and started rising up into the air. Zac took one last look at Voler and followed her.

'See you later, Agent Rock Star!' called Caz over her shoulder. 'Better luck next time!'

But Zac just grinned at her and waved.

Caz stopped mid-air. 'What are you smiling at?' she demanded.

'Nothing,' said Zac. 'I'm just thinking of all the awesome stuff I'm going to do with my new X-Beam.'

'What are you talking about?' Caz glared, holding up the plastic toad. 'I've got the blueprints right here!'

'Yeah, about that,' said Zac. 'When I put the plastic toad in my pocket, my SpyPad wirelessly transmitted the blueprints to GIB HQ! It's an automatic function.'

Caz stared at him, mouth open.

'And then it wiped all the data from the DSD,' added Zac. 'But don't worry, I'm sure your boss will find all kinds of useful things to do with a plastic toad!'

Zac spun his Chopper Suit around and flew away, laughing. Caz let out an angry shout and disappeared in the opposite direction.

Still chuckling to himself, Zac looked back towards the swamp. He saw Voler's jet shimmer into view above the island. His bodyguard must have been coming to rescue him.

I don't think Voler's game turned out quite according to plan, Zac thought. Then he felt his SpyPad vibrate in his pocket.

Excellent, he smirked to himself. *That's probably HQ calling to congratulate me.*

He pulled out the SpyPad. It was Agent Blizzard, the babysitter.

'Well done, Zac!' she said brightly. 'Now come straight home, please!'

'Thanks,' said Zac. 'Wait – what? Where are Mum and Dad?'

Agent Blizzard grinned in the screen of Zac's SpyPad. 'Your parents thought I did such a good job babysitting that they've decided to leave me in charge *again* tonight!'

Zac sighed. As if he needed a babysitter! *Well,* he thought, *at least flying home in my new Chopper Suit will be fun.*

'Oh, and I almost forgot,' said Agent Blizzard. 'You didn't finish your chores last night. When you get back, you've got some washing to fold!'

ZAC POWER

SKY HIGH

CHAPTER 1

CRACK!

The eight ball zoomed across the table and dropped neatly into the corner pocket.

'That's the game, Agent Rock Star!'

Zac Power sighed. His older brother, Leon, had just beaten him at pool. Again.

'You got lucky,' said Zac grumpily, tossing his pool cue down onto the table.

'Six times in a row?' said Leon. 'I don't think so.'

'But you never miss!' Zac snapped. 'How is that even possible?'

'It's all simple geometry, Zac,' said Leon smugly, reaching down to pick up a ball. 'Oh, and a bit of physics, of course.'

'Of course,' said Zac sarcastically. He thought privately that being the world's biggest nerd gave his brother an unfair advantage at this game.

Zac was a top spy at an elite agency known as the Government Investigation Bureau. Leon also worked for GIB, but he was a technical officer in charge of creating gadgets and organising missions.

Which means I'm still much cooler than he is, Zac reminded himself.

'Another game?' Leon asked, racking up the balls. 'Best seven out of thirteen? Tell you what, you beat me this time and I'll do all that vacuuming Mum asked you to do.'

'Fine,' said Zac. 'With a *normal* vacuum cleaner, though. No taking the easy way out with *that* thing.'

Zac pointed across the room to where a shiny purple gadget was sitting. The VacuuTron 5000. Leon had created it to cut down on cleaning time, and even Zac had to admit that it was a pretty cool invention.

If Leon's doing my chores, thought Zac, *he's going to do them the hard way.*

'OK,' said Leon. 'Deal. I'll even let you –'

But at that moment something started beeping. Leon reached into his pocket and pulled out a small electronic gadget.

The device looked a bit like a video game console, but Zac knew it was so much more than that. It was a SpyPad, every GIB agent's most useful tool. A video phone, a magnet generator, a laser, and a hundred other gadgets all in one.

Right now, a woman's face was staring impatiently back at Zac and Leon from the screen.

'Agent Shadow,' said Leon, straightening up. 'What's the word?'

'I've just got the green light from Headquarters,' said Agent Shadow. 'We've finally got enough intel to launch Operation Bug Eye.'

'Leon,' Zac began, 'what's —'

'About time!' said Leon, cutting Zac off. 'I've had the gear ready for almost a week!'

'Of course you have,' said the other agent, rolling her eyes. 'But we needed to wait for confirmation from WorldEye. Is Agent Rock Star up to the challenge?'

'Yup,' said Leon, glancing across at Zac. 'As long as there's no pool-playing involved.'

'Sorry?' said Agent Shadow, confused.

'Noth – ouch!' said Leon, as Zac kicked him in the shin. 'Nothing.'

'Very well,' said Agent Shadow. 'I'll leave you to brief him.'

'Great,' said Leon. 'See you.'

The image of Shadow flickered out.

'What was all that about?' Zac asked.

'Just finalising the preparations for your next mission,' said Leon happily.

'Preparations?'

Leon sighed. 'Your missions don't just organise themselves, you know. We're hard at work for weeks before you even get one of these,' he said, dropping a little silver mission disk onto Zac's palm.

'You're just not usually around to see it.'

'Oh,' said Zac. He'd never really thought about what went on behind the scenes at GIB. 'So what's this mission you've all been working so hard on?'

'How does firing a high-powered rocket into an invisible target sound?' said Leon.

'Piece of cake,' said Zac.

'Great!' said Leon. 'Did I mention *you're* the rocket?'

CHAPTER

Ten minutes later, Zac was speeding down the highway in Leon's Mobile Technology Lab. The MTL was a secret laboratory on wheels that was currently disguised as a furniture removal van.

Zac pulled out his SpyPad and slipped the silver mission disk inside.

CLASSIFIED

MISSION INITIATED 9 A.M.

An item of top-secret GIB technology has fallen into the hands of Professor Arthur Voler, a known enemy of the agency. GIB has determined that Voler plans to use this stolen technology to break into GIB's high-security vault in Bladesville at 9.00 a.m. tomorrow.

YOUR MISSION
- Infiltrate Professor Voler's hide-out.
- Prevent Voler from breaking into the GIB vault.
- Detain Voler until he can be placed under arrestl
~ END ~

Zac turned to Leon, who was standing at a workbench, tinkering with something that looked like a big metal backpack.

'Who is this Professor Voler guy?' he asked. 'I've never heard of him before.'

'Yeah, he's really secretive,' said Leon, without looking up. 'To be honest, we don't really know much about him. We don't even have a photo of him on –'

KA-BLAM!

Something exploded in front of Leon.

'What was that?' Zac shouted, ducking.

'Nothing!' said Leon quickly. 'Um, just running a final equipment check. Don't worry, I'm sure it won't do that when you're wearing it.'

'When I'm *wearing* it?'

'What we do know about Professor Voler,' Leon went on, quickly changing the subject, 'is that he's the most cunning thief GIB has ever come across. He travels the world, stealing rare objects and classified technology for his private collection. He's snatched stuff from BIG, from Dr Drastic, from a bunch of museums…'

'And now he's stolen something from us,' Zac finished.

'Right,' said Leon, pulling a little jar from his pocket, emptying it into his hand, and turning to Zac. 'Nine days ago, Voler got hold of a top-secret GIB prototype as it was being transferred to Headquarters from our research facility in Silicone Valley.'

'A prototype for what?' asked Zac.

'*This*!' said Leon dramatically, thrusting out his hand.

Zac stared down at Leon's hand. There was nothing in it. He raised an eyebrow. 'Professor Voler is stealing our air?'

Leon shot Zac a don't-be-stupid look and said, 'Scan it.'

Zac set his SpyPad to Magnify and pointed it at his brother's hand. The SpyPad locked onto a tiny spot on Leon's palm and zoomed in. There *was* something there after all.

Hovering just above Leon's magnified hand, tiny wings fluttering, was what

looked like a one-eyed insect, except that it was made out of metal.

'Oh,' said Zac. 'What is it?'

'This,' said Leon proudly, 'is a NanoCam, the latest in GIB surveillance technology. Tiny, remote-controlled spy cameras, invisible to the naked eye. They're amazingly fast, and because they're so small, we can send them –'

'Pretty much anywhere,' said Zac.

'Exactly,' said Leon. 'The down side is that they're incredibly expensive to produce. Right now, this is one of only two in the world. Professor Voler has the other one, and we need you to get it back.'

'And where does the exploding

backpack come into all of this?' Zac asked, looking sideways at Leon's workbench.

'Well,' said Leon, 'Voler likes to move around a lot, so he lives in the sky. His hide-out is an enormous jet plane, a bit like GIB's Hercules Transport.'

'So I'm going to fly up to him using the jetpack,' said Zac. 'Sounds simple enough.'

'Not quite,' said Leon. 'See, Voler has just outfitted his jet with some cloaking technology that he stole from BIG.'

'Wonderful,' said Zac. 'So that would be the invisible target you were talking about before?'

'Bingo,' said Leon. 'The good news is that the cloak was never meant to be used on anything as big as Voler's jet, so it's started to malfunction. We've caught a few glimpses of him making his way to Bladesville. It's not much, but it's enough to plot a course and get you aboard.'

'Assuming I don't explode on the way there,' muttered Zac.

CHAPTER

The Mobile Technology Lab pulled to a halt and Zac jumped out. Leon was right behind him, rolling the jetpack along the ground on a set of wheels. Enormous cornfields rose up on either side of the dirt road where they had stopped.

'Where are we?' Zac asked.

But Leon was busy tapping at his SpyPad.

'Quick,' he said, suddenly dashing off into the cornfield. 'This way!'

Zac followed, darting between the rows of corn. Green leaves lashed at his face.

He might have been much faster than Leon in a fair race, but here Zac had the disadvantage of not having a clue where he was going. He almost lost track of his brother a few times.

'OK, we're here,' said Leon, stopping as suddenly as he had started.

Caught off-guard, Zac lurched forward and almost bowled his brother over.

'Voler's jet will be passing over in a couple of minutes,' Leon said, still trying to catch his breath. 'We'll need to time

your launch exactly for this to work. Here, put this on.'

Leon rolled the jetpack over and Zac lifted it onto his back, staggering under the weight of it.

'Sorry it's so heavy,' said Leon, looking at his SpyPad. 'I needed to really cram in the fuel to get you up there.'

'It's fine,' said Zac, straightening up.

'As it is, there's only enough fuel for a one-way trip. You'll also need this to get you back down to earth,' Leon added, handing Zac a pocket-sized fabric package marked MICRO-CHUTE.

'Right,' said Zac, pocketing the parachute.

He grabbed hold of the two jetpack handles which now stretched out in front of him. Each one had a small, round button on the top. 'So, how does this work?'

'Hold down the right-hand button to activate the jets,' said Leon. 'Tilt the handles to steer.'

'And to stop?'

'There's a proximity sensor in the pack that will beep as you approach Voler's jet,' said Leon. 'As soon as you hear it, hit the left-hand button and brace for impact.'

'No worries,' said Zac confidently.

'Oh, that reminds me,' said Leon, pulling a fluffy little square of black cloth from his back pocket. 'Here, take this.'

'Huh?' said Zac. 'What do I need a tiny towel for?'

'It's a super-absorbent polymer I've been working on,' said Leon. 'It compresses water particles to a fraction of their usual size, so it can soak up around twenty times as much liquid as a normal kitchen sponge. It'll come in handy, trust me.'

'Uh-huh,' Zac said as he tucked the towel into his jeans.

'Seventy-two seconds to launch,' said Leon, eyes back on his SpyPad.

Zac glanced at his SpyPad.

11.30 A.M.

Leon paused, and then cleared his throat

loudly. 'There is one other little catch that I might not have mentioned.'

'You mean besides the fact that this jetpack could blow me to bit?' said Zac.

'Yeah,' said Leon. 'Here's the thing. Because Voler's jet is so high up, you'll need to really gun the jetpack to reach him. You'll be travelling at seriously high speed, too fast to pull out if something goes wrong. Either you hit the jet on your first try, or…'

'Or *what*?' Zac demanded.

'Or you keep going until you leave the earth's atmosphere and freeze to death,' Leon finished grimly.

'Great,' Zac said. 'So, no pressure then.'

CHAPTER

'OK, 30 seconds,' said Leon, glancing down at his SpyPad again. 'Remember, right button to activate, then wait for the beep and –'

'Yeah,' said Zac, gritting his teeth. 'Got it.'

'Got to run,' said Leon, turning around. 'Need to get clear of the blast radius. 20 seconds!'

And with that, Leon sprinted away through the cornfield.

Zac continued the countdown in his head. His white-knuckled hands gripped the jetpack controls. Only a few seconds left now.

3...

2...

1...

KA-BLAM!

It felt like the whole world exploded underneath Zac as he was catapulted skywards.

Looking down, Zac saw Leon staring up at him from the edge of a huge circle of charred-black earth — that take-off had burnt out almost half the cornfield!

Zac rocketed upwards. He kept his thumb down on the ignition and within seconds, the whole countryside was far beneath him.

Zac looked up, trying to catch a glimpse of the jet somewhere above him. But his eyes were watering from the wind rushing past his face, and he could barely see a thing.

Not that you'd be able to see a cloaked jet anyway, he reminded himself.

Zac had never travelled so fast in his life! His fingers tensed on the handles as he tried to keep his path as straight as possible, doing his best to ignore the way the jetpack rattled and shook.

Zac could see an enormous white cloud up ahead, and before he knew it, he'd flown straight into it. He had just enough time to get soaked from head to toe by the water vapour before he burst out of the top of the cloud, still surging towards his invisible target.

BEEEEEP!

Already? Zac thought to himself, as the proximity sensor sounded. Apart from the fact that he half-expected to get smashed to bits against the underside of Voler's jet, this was actually pretty fun!

BEEP-BEEP-BEEP

Zac released his hold on the ignition and slammed down on the left button.

KER-SPLAT!

A stream of sticky yellow goo shot suddenly from the top of Zac's jetpack, covering him from head to toe.

What the —

SMACK!

Zac collided with something huge and solid in the middle of the air, and stuck fast.

Despite being completely grossed out, Zac had to admire his brother's invention.

The gel from the jetpack was obviously some kind of high-tech padding. It had softened Zac's impact like an airbag, so he wasn't splattered across the hull of the jet. Not to mention sticking him fast so that he wouldn't fall straight back down to earth.

It was one of the most bizarre experiences Zac had ever had. There he was, flying upside-down through the air, glued to an invisible jet. And he looked as though he had just been sneezed on by a family of elephants.

Zac's eyes flashed to his watch.

Time to get inside. Pulling a sticky hand out of the goo, Zac felt his way around the surface of the jet until his fingers brushed past a large metal handle. He pulled on it and the door swung open with a click. Zac had to duck out of the way as several old-looking bags and boxes spilled out and went tumbling down to earth.

Must be the cargo hold, thought Zac.

Fighting against the gross slime that was still holding him to the underside of the jet, Zac slowly pulled himself up inside. He slammed the door shut behind him and stood up in the dark room.

Well, thought Zac, trying to flick the goo off his body, *I guess this explains the towel*.

He pulled the little black square out of his pocket and wiped himself down. Amazingly, the tiny towel soaked up every last drop of goo from his body without being squeezed out once.

Zac switched his SpyPad to Torch and shone it around the room.

At first it looked like there was no way out of the cargo hold, but then Zac pointed his SpyPad upwards and saw a small, round hatch set into the ceiling. He reached up and unscrewed the hatch, revealing a narrow tunnel with a ladder leading up one side. Pulling himself onto the first rung of the ladder, Zac clambered up into the interior of the jet.

At the end of the tunnel was another hatch, which creaked noisily as Zac twisted it open. He stuck his head up through the hatch and looked around.

Zac blinked as his eyes adjusted to the light. He had been expecting to find a high-tech computer room or a laboratory filled with bubbling chemicals.

Instead, he had just emerged into a

grand lounge room filled with beautiful antique furniture. The walls were hung with paintings and lined with shelves crammed full of trophies, trinkets and gadgets.

It looked like the kind of place that might be owned by a really rich guy in an old movie.

Suddenly, a voice broke the silence, making Zac jump.

'Ah, Zachary Power!' it said. 'Do come in. I've been expecting you.'

CHAPTER 5

Zac leapt out of the tunnel and whirled around. Smiling back at him from behind an ornate wooden table was a wrinkly old man. He was dressed in an expensive-looking suit and must have been at least 70 years old.

'Professor Voler?' said Zac uncertainly, wondering for a moment whether he'd boarded the wrong jet.

The old man nodded, and then gestured towards a large plasma screen on the wall.

Zac looked up at the screen and was startled to see an image of *himself* staring back. Zac raised his right hand. The Zac on the screen copied him exactly.

It was a live recording, coming from...

'That's right,' said Voler, as though reading Zac's mind. 'I've been using that marvellous NanoCam of yours to keep an eye on you. It's been buzzing around your ear for the last little while, transmitting video back to this screen.'

Zac could have kicked himself. Of course Voler had been expecting him!

He'd probably been tailing Zac with the NanoCam since he blasted off from the cornfield.

That meant the NanoCam was somewhere in this room.

If only I could see it! Zac thought.

The professor was holding what looked like a little remote control. He tapped at the remote with his thumb. Glancing back up at the screen on the wall, Zac saw the camera view pan around until it was pointed squarely at his face.

So that's what he's using to steer the NanoCam, thought Zac.

'I must say, you made quite an entrance!' said Professor Voler, in the tone of an old

man talking to his favourite grandson. 'And you're safely here now. Come and sit down, have some tea.'

'What did you say?' said Zac.

'Some tea, boy!' said Professor Voler, reaching for an ancient-looking teapot. As he did so, Zac noticed that Voler was wearing a strange, fingerless, silver glove. It had a small glassy bubble set into the palm.

The professor poured out two cups of hot, brown liquid and pushed one of them across the table in Zac's direction.

Whatever Zac had expected from Professor Voler, a hot drink had not been on the list.

'It is tea, Zachary,' said Voler, reading Zac's expression. 'I'm not trying to poison you. Go ahead and scan it if you'd like.'

Zac got out his SpyPad and scanned the tea cup. The reading came up instantly.

Contents: English Breakfast tea
Temperature: 81C
Toxins: None

'You see?' said Professor Voler. 'Now then, have a seat.'

'No,' said Zac.

'Come now, Zachary,' said Voler sternly. 'There's no need for that tone. What time is it?'

Zac checked his watch.

11.54 A.M.

'A few minutes shy of midday, correct?' said Voler. 'And as you're aware, I don't plan to break into the GIB vault until 9.00 a.m. tomorrow. Surely there's time for a spot of tea before we get down to business?'

Zac had no idea what to make of Professor Voler.

He had been expecting another crazy evil genius in a lab coat who would try to tie him up, or throw him behind a force field. Zac could handle bad guys like that.

But here was Professor Voler, a kindly old man, sitting calmly in his chair, offering him a cup of tea.

'Professor Voler,' Zac said firmly, trying to get this mission back on track. 'Please put the teapot down and step away from the table.'

'Come now,' said Voler, 'is this really necessary? After all, I've welcomed you into my home and –'

'I only came here to get back what you stole!' Zac retorted.

'Of course,' said Voler. 'But obviously I can't let you do that.'

'Let me?' said Zac, staring at the skinny old man. 'No offense, but you're not exactly going to put up much of a fight, are you?'

'Oh no,' Voler replied, shaking his head. 'I can't stand violence. Too messy.'

'Then what do you…'

Zac's SpyPad beeped suddenly, cutting him short. It was Leon. Zac reached down to answer the call.

FLASH!

A bright light flared suddenly in Voler's left palm. The SpyPad slipped from Zac's grasp and flew across the table.

'I'm sorry, Zachary,' said the professor, catching the SpyPad in his gloved hand and tossing it aside. 'But it really is very poor manners to answer your phone at the tea table.'

Zac's eyes were fixed on Voler's glove.

Suddenly, the professor seemed a whole lot less friendly.

CHAPTER

'Impressive, isn't it?' said Professor Voler, flexing his hand. 'Magnetic Field Gloves. I picked up a pair of them from a weapons designer in Nigeria.'

Zac glared at the professor. 'Picked them up?' he said. 'Stole them, you mean.'

'Well, yes, I suppose that's one way of looking at it,' Voler said with a nod.

'Like you stole the NanoCam,' Zac continued, taking a step towards the professor. 'Like you stole *all* of this stuff! You sit there acting all polite and friendly with your cups of tea and you think you're this big shot treasure hunter, but you're not! You're just a thief!'

'Zachary Power,' said Voler in his slow, calm voice, 'I will not tolerate such rudeness from guests in my home. Please calm down and drink your tea like a –'

'No,' said Zac.

Professor Voler pulled out what looked like a mobile phone, pushed a button and said, 'Alistair, may I see you in the lounge?'

A door hissed open behind Voler and

an enormous man stepped into the room.

'Alistair,' said Voler, 'Our guest is becoming difficult. Would you kindly teach him some manners?'

Alistair cracked his knuckles and nodded.

'I thought you said you couldn't stand violence!' said Zac as the man began moving towards him.

'I can't,' said Voler. 'Fortunately for me, he can.'

Zac turned and bolted out of the room. Bravery was one thing, but this guy could have snapped him in half with two fingers.

Other than the door Alistair had just come through, there was only one way out of the room. Zac dashed towards the other door and raced through it.

Slamming the door shut behind him and flipping the lock, Zac turned to find himself inside the jet's cockpit.

For a few seconds, Zac thought he had just found an easy way out of this mission. He could just take the controls and land the jet himself!

But a quick glance at the dashboard told him that everything was locked down and password protected.

Why can it never be that easy? he thought, looking for another way out.

A loud thud echoed from behind the cockpit door. Zac knew it wouldn't be long before Alistair broke the door down.

Zac looked at his watch.

Time to find another way out of here, he thought. *Maybe there's a —*

But then Zac caught sight of something that distracted him completely.

Sitting on top of a control panel, bobbing up and down in a jar of clear liquid, was a pair of *eyeballs*.

Zac's stomach lurched horribly.

What in the world was Voler doing with someone else's —

SHUNK!

Zac spun around. The cockpit door had just slid open a few centimetres and then stuck again.

'Almost there, sir,' said a gravelly voice from the room outside.

'Not to worry, Alistair,' said Voler calmly. 'He's got nowhere to go.'

But at that moment, Zac saw that there *was* somewhere for him to go.

Set into the floor of the cockpit was an air vent. It looked just about big enough for him to squeeze into.

Zac lifted up the air vent, revealing a dusty little tunnel. He stuck his head inside and started crawling.

SHUNK!

The cockpit door had moved again.

Far enough for Alistair to fit through? Zac wondered.

Breathing in, he squeezed his way further into the narrow tunnel, but his legs were still sticking out into the cockpit.

SHHHUNK!

Zac commando-crawled further into the tunnel. He was almost there! If he could just…

Suddenly, Zac felt a huge hand wrap around his ankle.

'Not so fast, Zac,' Alistair grumbled. 'You and I need to have a little chat.'

CHAPTER 7

With one enormous tug, Alistair wrenched Zac clear of the tunnel and tossed him up over his shoulder.

Zac tried to fight back, but the enormous man hardly seemed to notice.

Alistair carried Zac back across Voler's lounge room, through the doorway at the other end, and into a tiny room like a prison cell. It was empty except for a little wooden chair.

Zac landed with a thud as Alistair dropped him onto the floor in the corner of the room.

'Hand me your parachute,' said Alistair gruffly, holding out his hand.

'What parachute?' said Zac, playing dumb.

'Your brother handed you a small parachute just before you took off,' said Alistair matter-of-factly.

Zac realised that he had seen all this from the NanoCam.

'It's sitting in your left pocket,' Alistair added. 'Take it out and hand it to me.'

Zac pulled the Micro-Chute from his pocket and handed it to Alistair, who promptly ripped it in half like it was a piece of paper.

'Thank you,' Alistair said. Then he turned and walked out of the cell, shutting the door behind him.

A moment later…

HISSSSSSSSSS…

Zac looked around, searching for the source of the noise.

A stream of dark grey smoke was pouring steadily from a little black box on the roof of the cell.

That might be a sedative, thought Zac. *Knock-out gas.*

Seconds ticked by, and the smoke wafted lower and lower.

Zac ripped off his shirt, scrunched it up, and held it over his mouth and nose, trying to avoid breathing in the gas.

He searched desperately for another exit, but the only way out was through the doorway that Alistair was guarding. Zac could see the professor's bodyguard staring coldly back at him from behind the little glass window set into the door.

By now, the smoke was seeping through Zac's balled-up shirt, and he began to feel light-headed.

Zac's legs grew shaky underneath him and he lost his balance.

He tripped over, asleep before he'd even collapsed on the cold metal floor.

Zac groaned and slowly opened his eyes. As his vision began to clear, he realised that he was still lying on the floor of the little cell.

The smoke had gone now and looking up, Zac saw that Alistair was no longer standing guard outside.

He pushed himself up and glanced down at his watch.

8.13 A.M.

No! How could he possibly have been asleep for that long?

Professor Voler was going to break into the GIB vault in less than an hour!

Zac racked his brains for a way out of this cell, but his head was still a little hazy from the effects of the smoke.

He closed his eyes, trying to get his brain to start running at full speed again. He was usually so good at getting himself out of sticky situations, but... *That's it!*

An escape plan had suddenly dropped into Zac's head. He walked across the room and started hammering on the door.

'Hey!' he shouted. 'Hey, come here!'

After a few moments, Alistair's face reappeared on the other side of the glass.

He motioned for Zac to sit back down in the corner of the cell, then opened the door and stepped inside.

The bodyguard sat down on the little wooden chair.

Zac was surprised that the whole thing didn't just shatter into toothpicks under his enormous bum.

'What do you want?' said Alistair.

'I've made a decision,' said Zac.

'Oh?' said Alistair. 'What might that be?'

'I've decided there's no way I can overpower you,' said Zac.

'Yeah, no kidding,' the giant grinned, leaning back lazily on the chair.

'And if I can't fight back or escape,' said

Zac, slowly shifting his feet, 'then I might as well start doing what Professor Voler wants. I'm better off spending my time drinking tea out there rather than freezing my bum off on this cold floor, right?'

'You're smarter than I thought, kid,' said Alistair, tipping back even further on his chair. 'The professor is a brilliant man. One day you'll…'

Zac sprung forward in a flash and launched his full weight into Alistair's stomach.

Caught off-guard, Alistair fell backwards and landed with a thud on the floor.

'Didn't your teacher ever tell you not to lean back on your chair?' said Zac,

standing up and pulling out the little black towel that Leon had given him.

Zac held the towel over Alistair's head and squeezed it as hard as he could with both hands.

The yellow goo that Zac had mopped up earlier poured out of the towel in a huge stream, splashing across Alistair's face.

While Alistair struggled against the goo, Zac dashed through the doorway.

Then he slammed his hand down on the locking mechanism, sealing the giant inside.

To the right of the door was a small black button marked SEDATIVE.

Zac hit the button and shook his head at Alistair as fresh clouds of grey smoke filled the cell.

'Oldest trick in the book, Alistair.'

CHAPTER 8

Zac tore back up the hallway.

He was just about to burst back into Voler's lounge room when he noticed something moving around inside.

Rolling up and down the lounge room, like a guard dog on patrol, was a round, black object. It was about the size of a soccer ball and made out of metal.

Zac stopped at the doorway and watched the robotic ball. It was probably harmless, but just in case, he pulled off one of his shoes and tossed it into the room.

PEOOWW! PEOOWW!

Two blue lasers erupted from the metal ball at the first sign of movement. The shoe was a smouldering wreck before it hit the ground.

I guess this means I'm no longer welcome at the tea party, thought Zac, staring at the smoking remains of his shoe.

He needed a way to fool the motion sensor. In the far corner of the room Zac noticed an ancient-looking lounge chair piled high with fluffy cushions.

I wonder… He pulled off his other shoe and hurled it at the lounge.

PEOOWW! PEOOWW!

The twin lasers shot straight through Zac's shoe and into the pile of cushions. The cushions exploded, blasting a giant cloud of white feathers into the air.

And just as Zac had hoped…

PEOOWW PEOOWW PEOOWW!!

The metal security ball went nuts, spinning around frantically, trying to shoot down every last one of the feathers. There were hundreds!

The ball spun faster and faster, smoking, sparks flying, firing shot after shot, until…

BLAM!

A plume of black smoke burst out of the ball. It gave one final shudder and rolled over, broken.

Zac stepped cautiously out into the lounge room. Professor Voler was nowhere to be seen.

Zac glanced up at the big screen on the wall, hoping that this would give him a clue about where the NanoCam was.

But rather than a live picture of himself staring down from the screen, Zac now saw the high-tech city of Bladesville stretching out in front of him.

Enormous skyscrapers loomed as the NanoCam zoomed above the city streets towards the GIB high-security vault.

At least this meant Voler had given up watching Zac's every move. But now the NanoCam was outside the jet, and out of reach. *Which means that I need to get hold of Professor Voler's remote*, thought Zac, *and disable the camera from here.*

He checked the time.

8.41 A.M.

Nineteen minutes until Voler gets into the vault!

Ducking around behind the tea table, Zac found his SpyPad and stuck it back into his pocket.

He looked over at the doorway into the cockpit. It was shut tight again. That had to be where the professor had gone.

But it was no good just rushing in there without a plan. For all Zac knew, there could be ten more bodyguards as big as Alistair waiting for him.

Something bright and shimmering suddenly caught Zac's eye.

Sitting neatly folded on a shelf was a pair of the most disgusting-looking pants Zac had ever seen. They were bright pink and covered in horrible gold flowers.

A small label was stitched into the back:

Parachute Pants
Pull cord to engage chute.

A parachute! This could come in really handy if he needed to make a quick getaway. But if anyone saw him in these gross old hippy pants…

Zac rolled his eyes. *Come on*, he told himself, *time to be a professional*.

With a sigh, Zac picked up the big, baggy pants and slipped them on over his jeans. *Great*, he thought. *I look like a boy band drop-out*.

Zac continued searching. He still needed something to help him get hold of that remote. *Aha!*

Sitting on the next shelf across was a fingerless glove just like the one Voler had used to steal Zac's SpyPad.

Zac picked it up and slipped it onto his right hand.

Glancing back up at the plasma screen on the wall, Zac realised with a start that the NanoCam was no longer flying above the streets of Bladesville. It was zooming around inside a big, dark room.

Barely visible in the darkness was row after row of neatly stacked containers, each one stamped with the same logo: *Government Investigation Bureau*.

The NanoCam was *inside* the GIB vault.

CHAPTER

There was no time to waste.

Baggy parachute pants swishing loudly as he ran, Zac dashed across to the cockpit and opened the door. He was careful to hide his gloved hand behind his back.

Looking out the front window, Zac saw that the jet had now come to a stop, hovering high above the enormous city.

And there was Professor Voler, sitting in the black leather pilot's chair, gazing calmly out at the city. He held the NanoCam remote in his hand.

The professor turned in his chair as Zac took a step forwards. He looked down at Zac's flowery pants and gave a small smile.

For a moment, neither of them spoke.

'I don't get it,' said Zac, breaking the silence. 'How is the NanoCam going to help you break into the GIB vault anyway? It's just a camera!'

'It's already helped me immensely,' said Voler. 'As I'm sure you saw, the camera is small enough to squeeze under the door of the vault, so I've been able to have a good poke around and decide which items to take for my collection.'

'But that still doesn't get you inside,' said Zac.

'No,' said Voler. 'But these will.'

Professor Voler held up the jar that Zac had seen earlier. He reached in and pulled out the two eyeballs, rolling them around in his hand.

'Access to the GIB vault is protected by a retinal scanner,' Voler explained. 'Any person who wishes to enter the vault must first have their eyes scanned to prove they are permitted to go inside.'

'So you *stole* somebody's *eyes*?' said Zac, disgusted.

Voler burst out laughing. 'Gracious, is that what you thought? No, boy, these eyes are artificial replicas of the security guard in charge of the vault. I had them created using photos taken by the NanoCam.'

'So, what, you just hold them up to the scanner?' Zac asked.

Voler chuckled. 'Something like that. I told you it was a handy gadget.'

This was crazy. Zac didn't care if those things *were* fake. Any person who carried someone else's eyeballs around in a jar was just plain twisted.

'Where is Alistair?' the professor asked, as though he had just noticed that his bodyguard wasn't there.

'Back in that cell,' said Zac, trying not to sound too proud of himself. 'Out for the count.'

'Is he really?' said Voler. 'Goodness, you did well to overpower him. There aren't many who could do that.'

'Yeah,' said Zac. 'So just imagine what I could do to you.'

'You wouldn't harm an old man sitting in his chair?' Voler asked.

'No,' said Zac firmly. 'But I will take your remote.'

Zac stretched out his gloved right hand towards Professor Voler. He tensed his fingers, and the glassy bubble in his palm flashed to life.

The NanoCam remote flew through the air towards Zac. But before he could grab hold of it, Professor Voler leapt to his feet, and held out his own gloved hand in front of him.

The remote stopped dead in mid-air, caught between the two magnetic fields that were pulling it in opposite directions.

Zac strained his arm backwards against the magnetic attraction, but Voler was surprisingly strong for an old man.

For a full minute they stood there, both pulling with all their might. But the remote still quivered in the air between them.

Well, thought Zac, *this is going nowhere fast.*

Still pulling at the remote control with his gloved hand, Zac slipped his other hand into his pocket, pulled out his SpyPad and set it to Laser.

Then Zac waved his SpyPad in Voler's direction, sending the bright red laser beam flashing across his face.

The laser passed over the professor's eyes and, for a split second, he squinted and turned away.

It was all Zac needed. With one final flick of his wrist, the remote control zoomed into his hand. Zac dropped it to the floor and smashed it to pieces under his heel.

Voler straightened up, looking furious.

'Hand over the eyeballs,' said Zac.

The professor glared at Zac, and then dropped the fake eyeballs on the floor of the cockpit and kicked them across the floor towards him.

'Now,' said Zac, 'here's what you're going to do. You're going to take this jet and land it at the outskirts of the city. Then you're going to deactivate the cloaking device and wait patiently in that chair for the police to arrive.'

'As delightful as that sounds,' said Voler calmly, 'I must decline your offer. I simply cannot stand prison food.'

And before Zac had time to react, Voler bolted past him out of the cockpit.

CHAPTER 10

Zac thundered after Professor Voler, bursting back into the lounge room just in time to see him shoulder the GIB jetpack and disappear through the tunnel in the floor.

Losing no time, Zac dived down after the professor. He crashed down into the cargo hold and leapt to his feet again.

'I'd stay back if I were you,' the professor warned. He raised his foot high in the air and brought it down hard against the cargo hold's door.

CLANG!

The door flew off its hinges, tumbling down to earth.

Professor Voler turned towards the open hatch, pulling the jetpack's straps tight around his shoulders.

'Wait!' called Zac. 'There's not enough fuel!'

But it was too late. Voler had already thrown himself out into the open sky.

Without thinking, Zac sprinted across and jumped out after Professor Voler.

As Zac fell through the air, he guessed that he had less than two minutes before he got splattered on the footpath. Two minutes to catch Professor Voler and land safely.

Below him, Zac saw the professor fire up the jetpack to slow his fall, unknowingly burning up the last of his fuel.

Still free-falling, Zac was plummeting to earth much more quickly than Voler was.

Within seconds, he had closed the gap between the two of them.

Zac crashed down on top of the professor and grabbed onto his shoulders.

The impact sent the jetpack spiralling

out of control. Zac held fast to Voler, and the pair of them spun wildly around in a circle.

Zac twisted in mid-air, struggling to keep hold of Professor Voler. At the same time he was trying to avoid being burnt by the jetpack's exhaust.

'Let...*go!*' grunted the professor, struggling to shake Zac off his back.

The jetpack sputtered and shook as the fuel tanks ran dry.

'Listen!' Zac shouted against the rushing wind. 'You've used up all the fuel! If you don't hold on to me, you'll...'

But with one furious shove, Professor Voler broke free from Zac's grasp.

Zac reached out to grab him again, but it was no use. The professor was tumbling wildly towards the ground.

Zac had no choice. He pulled on the ripcord at his waist and activated the parachute pants.

The seat of Zac's pants suddenly billowed up and he slowed to a drift, his body hanging upside-down.

Unfortunately, this made it look like Zac's bum had been inflated to a hundred times its normal size.

Not exactly my most glamorous spy moment, Zac sighed.

It took several minutes for Zac to make his way to the ground. Finally he touched

down in a deserted alley, landing lightly on all fours. He stood up, pulled the cord again, and the pants slowly shrank back to normal.

Zac made his way out of the alley and into a busy Bladesville street.

People passing by stopped and stared at him. He couldn't really blame them. He *was* wearing really ugly parachute pants.

Zac gazed up and down the street, searching for some sign of Professor Voler.

He hated to think what he might find. After a fall like that, all that would be left of the professor would be…

'No way!' Zac whispered.

Smeared across the footpath up ahead

of him was a large puddle of something yellow and sticky.

Voler must have used the jetpack's cushioning gel to soften his fall! Zac doubted whether even Leon would have expected the goo to work that well.

Zac's SpyPad beeped suddenly. It was Agent Shadow.

'Agent Rock Star,' she said, 'We tracked your landing on WorldEye. Mission accomplished?'

'Mostly,' said Zac. 'Voler got away, but the NanoCam is safe inside the vault. And somewhere in the sky, there's a massive jet filled with stolen technology just waiting to be hauled back to HQ.'

'Excellent work, Agent Rock Star!' Shadow replied.

'Thanks,' said Zac.

'Oh, I nearly forgot,' Agent Shadow said. 'Your brother has asked me to inform you that he has decided to retire as undefeated pool champion of the family.'

It was clear from her confused expression that she had no idea what this message meant.

'He wishes to remind you,' Agent Shadow continued, 'That this means you have some vacuuming to do — *the hard way*.'

ZAC POWER

VOLCANIC PANIC

CHAPTER 1

It just isn't fair, thought Zac Power as he stared at the page in front of him. *I'm a secret agent! Why am I stuck here learning fractions?*

It was almost the end of a long school day, and Zac was counting down the minutes to the bell.

He may have been a highly trained member of the Government Investigation

Bureau, but that was all top secret. As far as his school was concerned, he was just an ordinary kid.

Zac's teacher, Mrs Tran, was away that day. They had a substitute teacher taking their class. Usually that was great because it meant the class got to do lots of fun stuff like art and PE.

But not this time. This new teacher had made them sit at their desks all day doing maths worksheets until Zac thought his brain would melt.

The new teacher's name was Ms Sharpe. She was tall and thin, and her jet-black hair was streaked with blue.

Zac didn't like her. There was something

about her smile that made Zac feel like he was in trouble, even though he was sure he hadn't done anything wrong. Not today, anyway.

Finally, the bell rang. Zac stuffed the worksheets into his maths book and got up to leave with the rest of the class.

'Just a minute please, Zac,' called Ms Sharpe. 'I need to rush off to an important meeting. Could you please close the blinds before you go?'

Zac sighed and walked back across the classroom towards the windows. He was about to pull the blinds down when suddenly, out of the corner of his eye, he saw something red and gleaming.

Sitting outside on the windowsill was a rock. It was about as big as Zac's hand, and it was glowing like it had just shot out of a volcano.

Zac looked around cautiously, but Ms Sharpe had disappeared.

His spy senses tingled. He opened the window and reached a hand out towards the rock.

For a moment, the rock burned red hot under his fingers. But then it grew cool and turned black.

A second later, the rock made a loud hissing sound and cracked open in Zac's hand, revealing a little silver disk. Zac's eyes lit up. *Excellent!*

A disk like this could mean only one thing – a new mission from GIB!

Zac smiled. His boring school day was about to get a whole lot more interesting.

CHAPTER

Zac raced to his schoolbag, and pulled out a small electronic tablet.

This was Zac's new SpyPad, the Pulsetronic V-66. It played video games, and it was also a phone, a code breaker, a laser, and just about everything else a spy could need.

Zac slipped the disk into his SpyPad.

CLASSIFIED
MISSION INITIATED 3 P.M.

*GIB has received a distress call
from Agent Hot Shot, who is stationed
on a small volcanic island called the
Isle of Magma.
Agent Hot Shock reposets that the island
has become extremely active, and may
erupt as soon as tomorrow afternoon.
He needs immediate assistance.
A cloaked GIB jet is waiting for you
behind the kindergarten
cubby house.*

*YOUR MISSION
- Locate and rescue
Agent Hot Shot.
~ END ~*

Zac pulled the disk out of the SpyPad and pocketed it. Leaving his schoolbag under his chair, he dashed down the hall and raced outside.

The playground was crawling with kids and their parents. Zac knew he'd have to be careful not to let anyone see what he was doing.

He slowed down and walked the rest of the way to the cubby house at the far end of the playground.

Hang on, thought Zac as he neared the cubby house. *If the jet I'm looking for is cloaked, that means it's going to be invisible.*

How am I supposed to climb aboard a jet that I can't even see?

But Zac's question was answered a moment later when he slammed into something cold and hard. 'Ouch!'

The invisible jet was right there in front of him.

Well, Zac thought as he rubbed his throbbing head, *at least I found it.*

Now came the hard part. He had to find a way inside.

Zac stared at the empty space in front of him. He was suddenly reminded of something he'd learnt in science last term about bats using echolocation to find their way in the dark.

This gave Zac an idea. Peering around to make sure that no-one was watching, he set the laser on his SpyPad to Multi-Beam, and pointed it in the direction of the cloaked jet.

Several sharp green beams shot out of the SpyPad. The laser beam bounced off the jet in front of him, lighting it up around the edges.

Zac moved the laser across the body of the jet until he found the cockpit door. He turned off the laser, pulled on the door handle, and climbed aboard.

The cockpit of the jet was small and cramped, not at all up to GIB's usual standard. Everything inside was black, except for the gleaming blue control panel.

Before Zac had even had a chance to run a pre-flight check, the door hissed closed and the jet slowly rose into the air above the school.

Autopilot, Zac thought to himself. *Sweet!*

Zac sat back in the hard plastic seat and breathed a sigh of relief. He was finally on his way!

Even though his jet was speeding through the air, Zac knew that the trip to the Isle of Magma would probably take several hours. It wasn't long before he started getting bored.

At first, it had been kind of cool to watch the city down below. But Zac had been on heaps of jet flights before, and he got tired of sightseeing pretty quickly. Anyway, he was out over the open ocean now, and it was getting dark, so there wasn't a whole lot to see. For a while Zac passed the time playing games on his SpyPad, but after his tenth round of *Ninja Nightmare* even that got boring.

Zac glanced at his watch again, feeling impatient.

9.24 P.M

He wished that something would happen, just to break the boredom.

And at that moment, something did.

A face appeared on the screen of his SpyPad. It was Zac's older brother, Leon.

Like the rest of the Power family, Leon

worked for GIB. But Leon wasn't a field agent like Zac.

He worked on GIB technology, and was in charge of some of the cool spy gadgets that Zac and the other GIB agents used to complete their missions.

'Zac, where are you?' Leon demanded. 'You're in big trouble with Mum for not having swept the leaves up from the driveway. And it's already past your bedtime!'

'Where do you think I am?' said Zac, surprised. 'I'm on a mission!'

On the screen of the SpyPad, Zac noticed Leon's raised eyebrow. 'Mission? What mission?'

'The mission to rescue Agent Hot Shot from the Isle of Magma!' said Zac. He was starting to get annoyed. 'The mission you sent me on with the cloaked jet!'

'Zac, what are you talking about?' Leon asked. 'You haven't been sent on a mission. Nothing's come through from HQ all day.'

'But I found a disk at school and...' Zac trailed off as he realised what must have happened.

'The mission disk!' Zac cried, pulling the little silver disk out of his pocket. 'It's a fake!'

Now Leon looked worried. 'Zac, you've got to turn that jet around right now and come home.'

'Right,' said Zac quickly. He reached out and started tapping at the sea of blue buttons in front of him.

Nothing happened.

'I'm locked out,' Zac said, trying not to panic. 'Nothing's working! The whole control panel is locked.'

'OK, calm down,' said Leon. He didn't sound very calm himself. 'Just, um, sit tight for a minute. I'll see what I can do.'

On the SpyPad's screen, Zac could see his older brother tapping frantically at his keyboard. Leon was trying to over-ride the jet's computer.

Suddenly the image of Leon on the SpyPad began to flicker.

'Leon,' said Zac, 'you're breaking up!'

'I know,' said Leon, his fingers still flying across the keyboard in front of him. 'It looks like someone's trying to jam our signal. I think —'

But the screen blinked and flicked off. Leon was gone.

Zac pulled the handle of the cockpit door, but it was sealed shut.

Wherever this jet was headed, Zac Power was going with it.

And there was nothing he could do about it.

CHAPTER 3

I've got to get out of this jet! thought Zac, as he looked around for something to help him escape.

If this had been a real mission, Leon would have given him a bunch of cool new gadgets to get him out of every sticky situation. But now all he had were the contents of his pockets.

He had two sticks of ParaGum, but even if he could open the door, what good would it do to parachute down into the freezing ocean?

He also had a couple of Marble Flares, but right now a flash of blinding light would only make things worse.

And then of course he was wearing his Turbo Boots, which would have been great...except that he hadn't refuelled them all week. They probably only had one good jump left in them.

At least Zac wouldn't have to wait long to find out where he was going. Looking up, he spotted something red and glowing ahead.

It was the mouth of a volcano. An extremely *active* volcano. And he was headed straight for it.

As the jet flew closer, Zac saw that the volcano sat in the middle of a tiny tropical island. The whole place looked completely deserted.

The jet whooshed to a stop, hovering just above the mouth of the volcano. Lava splattered upwards and lashed the jet on all sides.

After a few moments, a loud siren sounded and the jet began moving again.

Zac's heart skipped a beat. The jet was dropping. He was being flown down inside the volcano!

As the jet descended, Zac decided that he'd better be ready for anything. He pocketed the ParaGum and the Flare Marbles. Then he used the fake mission disk to back up the contents of his SpyPad, and slipped it inside his left sock.

Zac checked the time.

9.42 P.M

The jet plunged lower and lower, past brown rock and flowing lava, until it finally emerged into an enormous rocky cavern.

Zac blinked as he took in the sight. The cavern was filled with row after row of small black jets, at least fifty of them.

They were all identical to the one that Zac was sitting in.

That means there are lots of people down here, he thought.

Looking down, Zac saw streams of glowing red lava criss-crossing along the floor of the cavern, in between the black jets. The lava flowed through archways that had been dug out of the rock walls.

From where Zac was sitting, it looked like his jet was being lowered down into an enormous glowing spider web.

With a jolt, Zac's jet landed between two others. Steel hooks rose up from the ground and locked around the plane's undercarriage.

The cockpit door hissed open, and a wave of cool air washed over him.

Hang on, thought Zac. *Why is it so cold in here?* He was no scientist, but he was pretty sure volcanoes were supposed to be hot.

Zac jumped down to the floor. The cavern was eerily quiet, and his footsteps echoed loudly off the stone walls.

Then, in the distance, Zac heard hissing steam and whirring motors.

The sounds grew louder and louder until, finally, a line of three black vehicles whizzed through a tall stone archway.

The vehicles looked a bit like jet skis, but they were gliding down one of the lava channels on cushions of steam. A stream of icy water shot out of the back of each vehicle, propelling it forward.

The lava skis pulled to a stop, and two enormous women strode towards Zac out of the steam clouds. Both of them were dressed in matching black jumpsuits with a small lightning-bolt crest on the front.

Then a third woman stepped forward, wearing the same black uniform. She tossed back her shiny black hair.

Zac gasped. It was the substitute teacher, Ms Sharpe.

'Ah,' said Ms Sharpe with a cold smile. 'Zac Power. Welcome to BIG Central Command!'

CHAPTER 4

Zac stared at her. He'd heard of awful teachers, but this was ridiculous.

Ms Sharpe, a BIG spy?

BIG spies were the most evil in the business. They were GIB's greatest enemies. It seemed like every week there was some crazy new BIG plot for Zac to deal with. And now here he was at their Central Command.

'So,' Zac said, putting on a brave face, 'this was the important meeting you had to rush off to?'

'Glad you could make it,' said Ms Sharpe with a smile. She gestured towards the two women beside her. 'Allow me to introduce my fellow BIG agents, Hunt and Sloane.'

She clicked her fingers and the two women advanced on Zac.

BIG is right, thought Zac. These women were gigantic! If not for their uniforms, they might have been mistaken for a pair of gorillas.

Zac tried to dodge, but the big women were surprisingly quick. Hunt grabbed Zac around the shoulders, while Sloane snatched the SpyPad from his hand and tossed it to Ms Sharpe.

'Thank you, Sloane,' said Ms Sharpe, putting the SpyPad into her pocket. 'We can't have our hostage calling for backup now, can we?

'Now then,' she continued, 'I suppose you've already figured out why we've brought you here to Central Command, smart boy that you are.'

'If you think I'm ever going to join you…' Zac began angrily, but Ms Sharpe cut him off with a cold laugh.

'No, no, boy. We're not interested in you at all. What we want is money, and lots of it.'

'Oh, right,' said Zac. 'The usual.'

'Yes, Agent Rock Star, the usual,' Ms Sharpe said. 'World domination is a costly business, you know I'm sorry to say that you have done a fine job of thwarting all of our past efforts to lay our hands on GIB's money.'

'Yeah,' said Zac, 'I have, haven't I?'

'Indeed,' said Ms Sharpe. 'But not this time.'

'Oh yeah?' said Zac. 'What's so different about this time?'

'This time,' Ms Sharpe said coolly, 'you are the one we're holding to ransom. That's why I've sent my daughter to deliver a message to your agency's headquarters.

Either GIB delivers 15 million dollars to us by midnight tonight, or they never see their favourite agent again.'

Zac's eyes dropped to his watch.

10.02 P.M.

That left him less than two hours to get out of here!

But my mission isn't supposed to finish until tomorrow afternoon, he thought angrily. Then again, he should have known BIG would pull something like this.

'Wait a minute,' said Zac, playing for time. 'Did you say your *daughter*?'

'That's right,' said Ms Sharpe. 'Come to think of it, I believe you've met my darling daughter Caz before.'

Of course, groaned Zac.

Caz Rewop was another dangerous BIG agent. Zac had met her several times. She'd left him stranded inside a collapsing pyramid, had tried to brainwash him, and had even had a crack at infiltrating GIB Headquarters.

'Yes, my dear Caz gathered all kinds of information for me while she was working undercover at GIB,' said Ms Sharpe, 'including the designs for your mission disks.'

So that's how they made the fake disk, Zac realised.

It was time to make a move. Without a second's warning, Zac twisted under

Hunt's grip and slipped a hand into his pocket. Closing his eyes tight, he pulled out a Marble Flare and threw it to the ground.

The marble shattered, sending out a flash of blinding light.

'Argh!' shouted Hunt.

Zac felt her hands loosen their grip, and he wrenched himself free.

Opening his eyes, Zac saw that all three BIG agents had been blinded by the flare.

They were now staggering around, blinking madly and snatching at the air in front of them.

Zac sprinted across the cavern in the direction of the lava skis.

'He's getting away!' yelled Sloane. 'After him!'

'Fool!' came Ms Sharpe's reply. 'You can't even see! You'll run straight into the lava! Let the boy run, he's got nowhere to go.'

Zac leapt onto one of the lava skis, brought it around and with a burst of steam, shot through the nearest archway and out of the cavern.

CHAPTER 5

Zac zoomed on the lava ski down the channel of molten rock. He knew he needed a way to contact GIB for help.

More archways rushed by on his left and right, each one opening up into another cavern.

But every room was crawling with more BIG spies. There were hundreds of them, sitting at computers, watching surveillance screens, testing gadget prototypes.

As long as he was hidden by the cloud of steam from the lava ski, Zac thought he was probably pretty safe. But he couldn't just keep on riding up and down the corridors forever.

What I need, Zac decided, *is a disguise.*

He continued cruising down the lava stream, his eyes peeled.

Then he saw it – a little archway coming up on his left, with a sign above that read LAUNDRY.

At that moment, as Zac glanced down at the controls of the lava ski, a slight problem occurred to him.

Where on earth are the brakes on this thing?

The laundry room was coming up too fast!

Zac took a deep breath, and jumped off the lava ski, landing on a narrow stone ledge.

Up ahead, the unmanned lava ski flew out of control and smashed up into the side of the corridor, shattering a big glass pipeline that ran down the rock wall.

KER-SMASH!

Oops! thought Zac, as a torrent of water burst out from the shattered pipe. Panicked shouts echoed out from rooms nearby.

Zac ducked through the archway into the laundry room and held his breath.

'It must be Rock Star!' called a woman from down the corridor. 'He's escaped – Sharpe just sent out an alert! Quickly, this way!'

Moments later, half a dozen BIG spies ran past the laundry room archway and down the corridor.

When they were gone, Zac breathed a sigh of relief.

Digging through a nearby laundry basket, Zac found a BIG jumpsuit that was about his size.

Zac quickly realised it must have been the dirty laundry basket. And the suit belonged to a pretty stinky BIG agent. But there wasn't a whole lot of choice.

Zac slipped the suit on over his own clothes, and headed out into the hall.

After wandering the walkways for about 20 minutes, his eyes down to avoid attention, Zac heard a weird chugging sound coming from a room up ahead.

Looking around to make sure the coast was clear, he slipped inside to investigate.

The noise turned out to be coming from a big, bulbous pumping machine that looked like a giant mechanical spider. Huge glass pipes stretched out from each side of the machine. The pipes ran along the walls and back out the archway.

I must have smashed one of those pipes with the lava ski, Zac thought.

As Zac watched, the machine sucked up streams of brown, steaming water from the four pipes on the left, and then pumped clear, icy water out through the four pipes on the right.

So the pipes run through this whole place, thought Zac. *And all that cold water must be what keeps this place from burning up.*

Zac glanced around the rest of the room until he finally found what he was looking for – a deserted computer workstation.

He reached down into his sock and pulled out the disk that he had stashed there earlier.

Slotting the disk into the computer, Zac uploaded his SpyPad's communication software. His hands fumbled with the unfamiliar keyboard, trying to get the keys to work.

At last, the screen flickered and Leon's face appeared.

'Leon!' Zac hissed, keeping his voice low. 'I need your help. I'm at BIG Central Command and –'

'I know,' Leon interrupted. 'We got the ransom note about an hour ago. We've got a team working on tracking you down. But Zac, this is huge! BIG Central Command! GIB has been trying to find that place for years!'

Zac looked at his watch.

10.51 P.M.

'Yes, yes, it's all very exciting,' he said impatiently, 'but right now I wouldn't mind a hand escaping!'

'Right,' said Leon, and Zac could see him tapping on his keyboard. 'Hang on a minute, I might be able to use your connection to interface with the BIG network.'

'OK, cool,' said Zac, glancing back over his shoulder.

There was still no-one coming, but he probably didn't have much time.

'Wow,' said Leon, his eyes lighting up, 'this is an incredible system! I've never seen network security this advanced before! The encryption protocols they've put in place here are really —'

'Not now, Leon!' said Zac. Only his brother could get excited about computer security at a time like this.

'Right,' said Leon. 'Working on it.'

A second later, there was an electrical crackling. Then the lights in the room dimmed.

'Leon, was that you?'

'Yeah,' said Leon. 'At least, I think it was. I've sent through a virus to knock out the security cameras and the phone lines. That should keep you safe for a while. Now all you have to do is — whoa!'

'What?' said Zac.

'Nothing,' said Leon quickly.

'Leon!'

'Really, it's nothing,' said Leon. 'It's just that the volcano you're in is very… active.'

'I know,' said Zac. 'It was spitting lava when I got here.'

'That was nothing,' said Leon. 'BIG has set up a massive wall of electricity at the base of the volcano. Right now, that force field is holding back the worst of the lava flow. But if anything went wrong with the force field, the eruption would probably –'

'Blow the whole island apart!' Zac finished for him, a plan forming in his mind. 'Excellent!'

'What?' said Leon, sounding alarmed. 'Zac, no! It's too dangerous!'

But Leon was suddenly drowned out by a shout and the sound of approaching footsteps.

'Got to go!' said Zac, pulling his disk from the computer. The screen flickered out, just as Ms Sharpe and her bodyguards appeared in the doorway.

CHAPTER

'Hi,' said Zac, standing up. 'I was just leaving.'

'Oh, no you weren't,' said Ms Sharpe.

Hunt and Sloane lunged forward, but this time Zac was ready for them. He dived quickly to the ground, ducking under Sloane's legs.

Zac rolled across the floor and got to

his feet again, reaching into his pocket and pulling out a stick of ParaGum. It seemed a shame to waste it like this, instead of floating away with it, but if his plan worked…

The enormous women hovered around Zac. But he stood his ground, chewing frantically. As they drew nearer, Zac started blowing.

'Chewing gum, Agent Power?' said Ms Sharpe, raising an eyebrow as Zac's bubble grew bigger and bigger. 'I've heard of staying cool under pressure, but this is –'

BANG!!

'Argh!' cried Hunt and Sloane together as the ParaGum bubble exploded across their faces.

Zac grinned, weaved his way around Ms Sharpe and ran out of the room. For the second time that night, Sharpe's goons were left staggering behind, rubbing blindly at their eyes.

Zac raced down the corridor, hard rock on one side, bubbling lava on the other, and Ms Sharpe hot on his heels.

They were heading deeper into the facility now. Instead of laboratories and computer workstations, Zac saw that the stone archways they were passing led into smaller rooms with beds, bookshelves and small black teddy bears.

Zac glanced over his shoulder as he sprinted around a corner. Ms Sharpe was gaining on him, a steely look in her eyes.

Looking up ahead again, Zac saw a big metal door coming up on his right.

Was it unlocked? Would he be able to open it?

Zac stopped at the door and wrenched frantically at its cold metal handle.

Come on, come on . . . Yes!

It took both arms to heave the door open. Zac dived inside and slammed the door shut behind him with an enormous crash of metal on metal. Then he threw down the deadlock.

He heard Ms Sharpe hammering furiously on the other side of the door, but she wasn't getting through in a hurry.

I'm safe for now, he thought, glancing at his watch.

11.08 P.M.

Zac had a look around the bedroom. *The bad news,* he thought to himself, *is that there doesn't seem to be another way out of here.*

Ms Sharpe had given up banging on the door, but all that meant was that she had probably gone for help.

He turned and looked around at the room he'd locked himself into. It was another bedroom, but this one was much nicer than the others he had just been running past.

There was an expensive-looking rug on the floor, a huge canopy bed at one end, and a wooden writing desk at the other.

Zac didn't have to look far to find out whose room he was in. There was an ID card and a little photo frame on the desk.

Smiling up at him from the picture frame were Ms Sharpe and her daughter, Caz. They were sitting on a park bench, eating ice-creams like a perfectly normal, non-evil mother and daughter.

Still, thought Zac, *there's something really creepy about that picture.*

'Zac! Hey, Zac!'

He jumped and spun around. *Where is that voice coming from?*

'Zac! Over here!'

Zac crossed over to the other side of the room, and then he saw it. Sitting on the end of Ms Sharpe's bed, blending in almost perfectly with the bedspread, was a shiny black iPod.

And it was talking to him.

CHAPTER

You've had a long day, Zac told himself sternly. *You've had a long, hard day, and now you're tired and you're imagining things. You know iPods can't talk.*

'Are you there, Zac?' said the voice.

'I know iPods can't talk!' Zac snapped.

And now you're arguing with a music player, thought Zac. *Fantastic.*

'What?' said the voice. 'Oh, right. No. Zac, it's me – Leon.'

'But –'

'Hold on a minute,' interrupted Leon, and a moment later his face appeared on the iPod screen.

'There we go.'

'Oh,' said Zac, finally catching on. 'But hold on. How are you doing that?'

'All the technology here is on a wireless network,' said Leon proudly. 'Including the iPods. Now that I've hacked into the system, I can pretty much go wherever I want.'

Zac grinned. For a nerd, Leon was pretty cool.

'Anyway,' Leon continued, 'I tracked the path of that jet you came in on, and used it to plot a course for the back-up team to come and rescue you. They're coming out in the Squid.'

'In the what?' said Zac.

'Oh, it's really cool!' said Leon excitedly. Clearly, the Squid was one of his own inventions. 'Wait until you see! Anyway, the back-up team is almost there, so all you need to do is get back out of the volcano and –'

'I can't leave yet,' said Zac. 'I still need to bring down the force field and destroy this place!'

'No, you have to get out of there!' said

Leon. 'I don't like BIG any more than you do, but it's too dangerous.'

'Leon, I can do this!' said Zac, almost shouting now. 'Look, there are plenty of jets up there for everyone to get away in. No-one will get hurt. All I have to do is stop BIG from using this place for evil.'

Leon sighed. 'I can't talk you out of this, can I?'

'No,' said Zac simply, 'you can't. Now, are you going to help me find the force field or aren't you?'

'Honestly,' Leon muttered as he went to work at his keyboard, 'you're so annoying when you get like this.'

Zac just smiled to himself.

'OK,' said Leon after a few moments, 'I have good news and bad news.'

Zac sighed. *Why is there always bad news?*

'The good news,' Leon continued, 'is that you won't have to go far to find the door that goes to the force field generator.'

'Great!' said Zac. 'Where is it?'

'You're standing on it.'

Zac stared down at his feet. Then he reached down and heaved aside the heavy rug, uncovering a little wooden trapdoor.

Well, thought Zac, *that explains why Ms Sharpe's bedroom needs a giant metal blast door.*

'Excellent!' said Zac. 'OK, what's the bad news?'

'The bad news,' said Leon, 'is that there

are about 20 BIG agents on the other side of that bedroom door, and they're approximately 30 seconds away from breaking it down.'

CHAPTER 8

BANG!

Zac's ears rang as something large and heavy crashed into the other side of the big metal door, shaking it on its hinges.

Time to go, thought Zac. He slipped the iPod into his pocket and bent down to grab hold of the brass handle at the edge of the trapdoor.

BANG!!

The whole room shook as Ms Sharpe and the other BIG agents took another shot at the door.

Zac tugged at the handle and the trapdoor lifted up easily, revealing a narrow, pitch-black tunnel. He bent down to peer inside, but couldn't see a thing.

BANG!!!

Zac looked back over his shoulder. The door was beginning to buckle.

Ms Sharpe's voice rang out from the other side of the door. 'Almost in!'

I'm almost out, Zac thought to himself, pulling a Marble Flare from his pocket. He tossed the marble down through the opening in the floor, and a moment later the whole tunnel burst into light. Careful not to look directly at the flare, Zac could see a series of thin metal bars forming a ladder down into the tunnel.

He tested the top rung with his foot and began to climb down.

No sooner had Zac's head and shoulders bobbed down into the tunnel than –

BANG!!!!
KER-SMASH!

The giant metal door exploded out of its frame and came crashing down on top of the tunnel entrance.

'Told you,' said a small voice from Zac's pocket.

Zac kept climbing down, and soon he'd reached the bottom of the tunnel. Shielding his eyes from the Marble Flare still burning at his feet, he peered around.

Now where do I go?

He didn't have to look far. From the end of a tunnel to his right, Zac heard a distant crackle of electricity. He could also see bright flashes of red, blue and purple.

Zac raced down the tunnel, which turned out to be longer than it looked.

As he drew closer to the force field generator, the fierce electrical crackling grew louder and louder.

Finally, Zac emerged from the passageway into what turned out to be another enormous cavern, almost as big as the jet hangar at the volcano's entrance.

Zac's stomach plummeted as he looked up at the far wall of the cavern, and saw that it wasn't a wall at all. It was a surging sea of molten rock that extended for 50 metres in each direction.

The only thing stopping all that lava from spewing out and flooding BIG HQ was the paper-thin force field being projected across the cavern by a little generator in the corner. It was freaky. It was kind of like standing in front of one of those enormous shark tanks at the aquarium.

And here I am, about to break the tank's glass, Zac thought.

He glanced down at his watch.

11.53 P.M.

Not that the ransom deadline would matter if his plan worked.

Zac ran to the computer station. A giant sign was posted on the wall above it.

DANGER
FORCE FIELD
GENERATOR

NO ACCESS.

This generator operates under a 5-minute emergency lock-down protocol. In case of emergency, agents will have 5 MINUTES to leave BIG Central Command.

Zac glanced down at the little touch screen on the side of the generator, then pulled the iPod out of his pocket.

'Leon!' he said. 'The generator is password protected! I need a code to shut it down!'

'Right,' replied Leon. 'I'm on it.'

But at that moment, Ms Sharpe burst into the room.

Zac spun around and peered down the passageway behind her. 'Where's Hunt and Sloane this time?'

'Luckily for you, they were too, er, *big* to fit through the tunnel,' Ms Sharpe said.

I bet they were, thought Zac.

'Well, you'd better head back up there

yourself,' he said. 'In a few minutes, it's going to get pretty hot in here.'

Ms Sharpe laughed. 'I don't think so, Agent Rock Star. That generator is protected by state-of-the-art BIG security. There's not a spy in the world who could shut it down.'

DING!

A large blue button appeared on the touch screen and an electronic female voice could be heard over the crackling force field.

PASSWORD ACCEPTED.
TOUCH SCREEN TO DEACTIVATE
GENERATOR.

'Not a spy in the world,' said Zac proudly, 'except for my brother.'

Ms Sharpe looked like she'd just been punched in the stomach.

'Zac,' she said, sounding panicked, 'please, be reasonable! Let's talk about this like civilised people!'

'Right,' said Zac dryly, 'like the kind of civilised people who kidnap each other and trap them inside a volcano. I don't think so.'

He thrust out his hand toward the touch screen.

'WAIT!' cried Ms Sharpe.

Zac's finger froze, millimetres from the blue button.

'What?'

'Your grandfather!' Ms Sharpe said desperately, a mad gleam in her eye. 'I know you'd love to find him! I can help you. Come with me, Zac, and we'll find him together!'

For a long moment, the two agents stared at each other in silence. Zac's grandpa had disappeared on a jungle mission many years ago. Zac and his family had never heard from him since.

Then Zac broke the silence. 'My grand-father spent his life putting people like you out of business!'

And with that, he lifted his hand and slammed it down onto the touch screen.

'Time to move!' said Zac, and he bolted past Ms Sharpe and back through the passageway.

CHAPTER 9

WARNING: FORCE FIELD DEACTIVATION IN 5 MINUTES.

For a few seconds, Ms Sharpe stood frozen on the spot, staring at the force field. Then she turned on her heels and raced after Zac.

Reaching the end of the passageway, Zac clambered up the ladder and out into Ms Sharpe's bedroom.

Leaping over the battered metal door, he darted out of the room and back along the stony corridor.

Up ahead, BIG agents were streaming out into the corridor through the archways on either side, and sprinting off towards the jet hangar.

Zac could hear Ms Sharpe running behind him.

WARNING: FORCE FIELD DEACTIVATION IN 4 MINUTES.

Zac rounded another corner. Halfway down the corridor, he saw a lava ski lying abandoned on its side. He raced over, picked it up, and hoisted it down into the lava stream.

Hopping aboard, Zac took one last look around and saw Ms Sharpe staggering up the corridor, clearly out of breath.

WARNING: FORCE FIELD DEACTIVATION IN 3 MINUTES.

Zac sighed. Sometimes being a good guy was a pain in the butt.

'All right,' he said wearily, as Ms Sharpe caught up. 'Get on.'

'Huh?' she began. 'Why would you…?'

'Look, do you want to get out of here or not?' Zac snapped. 'Get on!'

Zac gave Ms Sharpe about three seconds to climb onto the lava ski behind him, then he gunned the accelerator. In a flurry of steam, they raced along the lava stream towards the hangar.

The lava ski bucked and bounced beneath Zac's feet and it took every ounce of his game-playing reflexes to keep it from spinning out of control.

WARNING: FORCE FIELD DEACTIVATION IN 2 MINUTES.

'That was a really nice thing to do,' Ms Sharpe said suddenly.

'What?' said Zac absently, struggling to control the speeding vehicle.

'Sharing your lava ski with me,' said Ms Sharpe, 'was a really nice thing to do.'

Zac rolled his eyes. 'Yeah? Well, lucky for you I'm the nice type.'

Zac sped around one final corner and

burst through the tall archway and out into the jet hangar.

'Jump!' yelled Zac, and he dived off the lava ski onto the stone floor. Ms Sharpe thudded to the ground next to him. A second later –

KER-SMASH!

The lava ski exploded against the cavern wall.

'Those things do have brakes, you know!' Ms Sharpe grunted.

'Right,' said Zac. 'Next time, you can be the driver and I'll be the evil kidnapper.'

Ms Sharpe moved to get up, but Zac stopped her with a look. 'I'll have my SpyPad back now,' he said, his hand out.

Ms Sharpe snarled and handed over the SpyPad.

WARNING: FORCE FIELD DEACTIVATION IN 1 MINUTE.

They leapt to their feet, looking around the enormous cavern. The same thought entered both of their heads.

Only one jet left. And there was no way both of them could fit inside.

'Take it!' said Zac.

'What?' said Ms Sharpe, as though she thought Zac was trying to lure her into some kind of trap.

'Take the jet!'

'But –'

'Ms Sharpe!' Zac shouted. 'You were a

lousy substitute teacher and you're an even lousier spy! The only way you're going to make it out of here is in that jet! Now get in there before I change my mind!'

Casting him one last suspicious look, Ms Sharpe bolted across the cavern and climbed up into the jet.

The cockpit door hissed closed and the sleek black aircraft rose quickly up through the volcano towards the safety of the open sky.

'OK,' Zac muttered to himself, 'time to get out of here.'

WARNING: FORCE FIELD DEACTIVATION IN TEN SECONDS.

Zac knew he had only one chance to escape.

NINE...

He ran across the floor of the cavern,

EIGHT...

leapt across the last lava stream in his path,

SEVEN...

positioned himself directly below the mouth of the volcano,

SIX...

crouched down on the ground,

FIVE...

pulled up the leg of his jeans,

FOUR...

reached for the green button on the side of his Turbo Boots,

THREE...

held his breath,

TWO...

and pushed the button.

ONE.

But absolutely nothing happened. *That's not good,* Zac thought as the whole cavern began to shake.

FORCE FIELD DEACTIVATED.

CHAPTER 10

He knew his Turbo Boots were running low on fuel, but surely they had enough in them for one more jump. He pressed the button quickly with his finger.

Suddenly, lava spewed into the hangar from all sides, gushing in through the stone archways and blasting them apart with the force. Waves of molten rock swept across the floor of the hangar, melting everything in their path.

In seconds, the whole cavern would be a swirling ocean of fire, and Zac would be in it. The waves were only metres from him now. Only centimetres. Then –

KA-BLAM!

The twin rockets in his Turbo Boots roared to life, and he was thrown upwards.

He was tearing his way up through the throat of the volcano now, racing past the rock walls at an insane speed.

Zac looked down and saw hot lava rushing up below. The rockets in his shoes sputtered as the Turbo Boots ate up the last of their fuel.

Come on, come on! Zac thought, willing the boots to keep going. *Almost there!*

And then he was clear. Zac leant forwards and the rockets propelled him out over the ocean.

A moment later, the volcano erupted into fire and ash. *Now that,* Zac thought to himself, *was a close one.*

Then, with a final splutter, the Turbo Boots gave out and Zac began falling towards the dark sea.

Zac reached into his pocket and snatched up the last piece of ParaGum. Then he crammed it into his mouth, and chewed as hard as he could.

He was tumbling head over heels

through the air now, towards the churning ocean below.

Sticking out his tongue, Zac blew into the ParaGum with all his might.

FWOOSH!

Zac's bubble was caught in an updraft and he began to drift lazily toward the water below. *Phew!*

Now where's my back-up? Zac wondered. *I thought Leon said —*

THWACK!

Suddenly, an enormous tentacle darted up from the water and caught Zac around the middle, bursting his enormous ParaGum bubble.

'Hey!' Zac shouted out loud.

It looked like some sort of giant octopus or something, except that it was obviously mechanical.

Padded metal tentacles, like the one that had just grabbed Zac, waved in all directions, and…

Suddenly, it dawned on him.

So this is the Squid, Zac thought admiringly.

He had to hand it to his older brother. Leon certainly was creative!

A hatch opened in the top of the Squid. The tentacle holding Zac lowered him inside, where Leon was waiting with the rest of the GIB back-up team.

'Need a lift?' Leon grinned.

'Yeah, thanks,' said Zac. 'Nice ride you've…'

But he trailed off when he saw his parents sitting there.

'What are you doing here?' Zac demanded, as his dad pulled him in for a hug.

'We wanted to make sure you were OK!' his mum replied. 'BIG Central Command! I never thought –'

'I told them you'd be fine,' Leon apologised. 'But they insisted on coming as back-up.'

Zac groaned. *This is so embarrassing!*

'I'm very proud of you,' said Zac's mum, finally releasing him from a hug almost as tight as the Squid's tentacles. 'Now, let's get you home. Don't you think I've forgotten about you sweeping the driveway!'

'But…' Zac began. Surely blowing up BIG's volcano had earned him a bit of time out?

'But nothing,' his mum said sharply. 'You might have saved the world from BIG, but that doesn't mean you get out of doing your chores at home!'

'Fine,' Zac sighed. There were some things even a world-class secret agent couldn't escape.

JOSHIE HECTIC:
NOT EVEN THE WORLD'S MOST ADVANCED DROID CAN KEEP HIM OUT OF MISCHIEF!

When an **incredibly sophisticated droid** arrives at his house one morning, Joshie thinks it's pretty cool. The **not-so-cool** thing? It's programmed to babysit Joshie while his mum is at work. But Joshie **DOES NOT NEED** a babysitter, so things are going to get pretty **hectic** around here ...

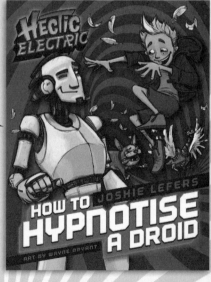

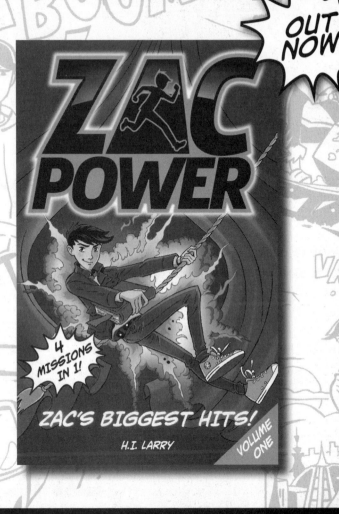